The Bloodhound's Story
Book 2 of
The TRACKERS SERIES

Mickey Morningglory

MICKEY MORNINGGLORY

Patent Print Books

Panama City Beach, Florida

MIST is a work of fiction. The characters and events portrayed in this book are fictitious.

Copyright ©2017 by Mickey MorningGlory

All rights reserved. Except as permitted under the U.S. Copyright Act of 1976, no part of this publication may be reproduced, distributed, or transmitted in any form or by any means, or stored in a database or retrieval system, without the prior written permission of the publisher.

Published by PATENT PRINT BOOKS
www.patentprintbooks.com

PATENT PRINT BOOKS and the fingerprint colophon are registered trademarks of PATENT PRINT BOOKS

First Edition: August 2017

ISBN 978-0-9850731-1-4

Library of Congress Control Number: 2017918244

Printed in the United States of America

Edited by Ann W. Carns

10 9 8 7 6 5 4 3 2 1

*In memory of
Dr. Wilbur A. Middleton ~
My inspiration, my hero, my father.*

FOREWORD

The number seven has always been special in literature and history. What if you discover you are the seventh son of a seventh son? What potential wisdom, force, or power have you inherited from your ancestors? How can you learn to express yourself as a tracker? And will you serve as a force for good or succumb to the selfish lure of evil?

A growing, crowded, exciting society can be found almost anywhere in present-day America. This author produces human characters who live, love, and compete for power and success in the pluralistic State of Florida. Power politics, big-time sports, and mystical dimensions of extra-sensory time travel capture the reader's interest. Unexpected themes drawn from ancient value systems, from Hispanic culture, and from Native American intrigue permeate the more normal local, secular culture in Florida's capital city and its environs. Every reader will identify with the pathos of vicious kidnapping, of fortunes made and lost, and of intimate love so close and yet so far away.

Mickey MorningGlory writes in a crisp, sharp, and brisk tempo. Her compelling characters capture your attention and the suspense of their intricate involvements, both virtuous and vicious, will keep you glued to the page until you arrive at the surprising conclusion. And then you will quickly ask for the next installment in this well-planned series which promises to continue to draw us into the amazing adventures of these exciting trackers.

~ Robert G. Newman, Ph.D.
A.J. Humphreys Professor of Religion
The University of Charleston

CONTENTS

Prologue	Tallahassee, Florida~1992 / 1
Chapter 1	Sunday, 1992 / 5
Chapter 2	Scents of Loss / 22
Chapter 3	Training / 31
Chapter 4	Agony and Ecstasy / 45
Chapter 5	To Tampa / 55
Chapter 6	Fawn Lightfoot / 65
Chapter 7	Cedar Woman's Gifts / 84
Chapter 8	In Sickness / 96
Chapter 9	Tracking the Drug / 105
Chapter 10	Country Boys in the City / 115
Chapter 11	Making Scents / 125
Chapter 12	Awakening / 140
Chapter 13	On the Scent Trail / 150
Chapter 14	Rain and Shine / 167
Chapter 15	Old Friends, New Family / 178
Epilogue	The Keeper / 189
Appendix	Language Translations / 194
Preview	Kachina: The Snapshot's Story / 199

PREFACE

MIST was not going to be the next book in *The Trackers Series*. It was to be Raven's story. But you know how stubborn those Lightfoot boys are. While I struggled to draft *KACHINA,* Dane Lightfoot kept invading my sleep wanting his tale told. So, Raven agreed to take a back seat until I completed *The Bloodhound's Story*, and now she's glad she did! You'll see why very shortly.

~ Mickey

ACKNOWLEDGMENTS

I want to thank those who had a part in the inspiration and completion of this book (in alphabetical order):

Ann C., Felecia B., Guy T., Helen S., Jan V., Katie N., Lisa B., Margaret K., Mike C., Robert N., Stephen N., Wayne B., my editor, my publisher, and especially my family.

INTRODUCTION

Ecstasy...the *"Love Drug"*. Even its name invokes thoughts of *euphoria*. Users claim it brings feelings of extreme joy, closeness, trust, exhilaration—emotions that blend well with the "dance-all-night" atmosphere of rave parties.

Unfortunately, this drug-induced "excite-ment" often causes the user to drop his or her guard, trusting those who cannot *always* be trusted, giving rise to sexual promiscuity, even rape; ingesting other drugs, usually in dangerous or deadly combination; and oftentimes resulting in permanent psychological or physical injury or death.

Over the years, I've found that the use of these dangerous drugs crosses all social divides, all ages, all races...it honors no one. During my thirty-five-year law enforcement career, on too many occasions I've had the unpleasant duty of notifying friends, parents, even spouses, of the arrest, serious injury or death of their loved ones due to illicit drugs. It is a duty that I never wanted and, with each case, *never* forgot.

~ Guy Tunnell
Retired Sheriff, Bay County, FL
Former Commissioner,
Florida Department of Law Enforcement

PROLOGUE
TALLAHASSEE, FLORIDA~1992

She could not have been happier. Everything was going so well. The music was loud; the beat was strong and pulsating. The lights were incredibly bright and colorful, and they seemed to dance with the tempo of the music. His hands on her bare shoulders gave off heat waves, and it felt good. She gyrated her hips and gave him her best "come-on" look.

He pulled her closer, and they danced as one unit, swaying and bumping to the undulating rhythm of the song. He pushed her hair away from her neck and leaned in to her, breathing in the intoxicating scent of her perfume as he moved his mouth beneath her ear. Pulling back, he licked his lips. They tingled—not pleasantly.

She wrapped her arms around his waist. Grasping the back of his shirt, she raised herself up on her toes to meet his kiss. *Hot,* she thought. *So hot.* She giggled at the double entendre, and then she frowned. He was so incredibly attractive, and she was anxious to be with him, but she was burning up. Sweat beaded beneath her nose and dried immediately, leaving a salty, crusty residue; her lips felt parched, chapped.

"I need something to drink," she gasped, pulling away from him. The room was an oven; she had to cool down.

He agreed, taking hold of her hand and weaving through the dancing throng toward the bar. He suddenly felt he was dragging her—like dead weight. *Why is she hanging back?* Turning around, he felt the room spin, and he shook his head to clear his vision. *Where is she? There.* She seemed yards away, but, looking down, he noticed they still had their hands clasped.

She went to her knees without warning, panting, staring wide-eyed at him. *What's happening?* She panicked. *Help me!* She tried to call out, but her tongue was thick, dry, stuck to her teeth. Her eyes felt like sand in their sockets.

He watched her fall over to her side. It was slow, like a stop-action movie. Her eyes never left his, all the way down to the floor. Then the room tilted away, became dark and quiet, and he was gone, too.

* * *

Thirty miles away, Dane Lightfoot came awake slowly, his nose filled with the scents of floral, jasmine, musk, and something he couldn't identify. It was overpowering, and he jammed his index fingers into his nostrils. Pressing on the cartilage between his fingertips, he breathed rapidly in and out through his mouth. He removed one finger, then the other, and took a slow, cautious breath. *Perfume—very high end, complex, smells expensive.* He took another, deeper breath. *Sweat, stale body odor.* Another breath. *What IS that?*

Suddenly, he was overwhelmed with thirst. Flinging back the covers, Dane jumped up from the bed and bounded into the kitchen. Grabbing a plastic cup from the dish drainer, he filled and drank a total of four glasses of tap water before he felt quenched.

The mysterious smell was gone now, and Dane perched on the bar stool, absently running his finger around the top of the cup. *Somebody's dead,* he decided, *and it wasn't pretty.*

* * *

Hundreds of miles away, my eyes fly open, and I stare at nothing. I don't know the young couple, but I know Dane, though I've only recently come to learn of him. He is my brother—the one who just returned from beyond the veil of death.

I am Luna—short for *Ojos del Luna* (as my village family calls me); *Hvresse Torwv* (as my Creek Indian mother calls me). Both names mean the same—Moon Eyes. Mother says my eyes are so blue they are almost white, and that is why I am blind. But in my dream travels, I can see everything. I often travel great distances as I play my flute, and in my travels, the world is vivid and colorful, with keen sensory perceptions of sound and smell.

I am a "Story Keeper." I remember in great detail what I see on my journeys. The stories I tell are not mine, but I keep them in my memory always, as do I keep all the other stories related to this group of people whose lives intersect mine in a strange and unexplainable way.

This one is his—the Bloodhound's story. It begins the night my brother Dane awakes smelling death.

CHAPTER ONE
SUNDAY, 1992

LIAHONA "LEE" THISTLESEED'S HOUSE IS BUZZING with excitement today. The Mohawk leader of the elite clairvoyant Trackers Team is in his element, with his family and friends all around him. The three Thistelseed boys—Cy, Bill, and Kenny—clamor for attention from Graham Skysong, the Navajo clairaudient who can imitate any voice he hears. Graham entertains them by doing impressions of Porky Pig, Daffy Duck, and whatever cartoon characters they call out.

"Nyaaaaahhhh! What's up, Doc," Graham quips in the voice of Bugs Bunny. In his lap, seven-year-old Shelly—Lee's youngest child—squeals loudly as he tickles her.

Lee's wife, Wren, bustles about, setting places and putting the finishing touches on the food. The oldest daughter, twenty-four-year-old Shinehah, sets up a couple of card tables in the family room for the younger kids.

Nicknamed "Shine," she looks very much like her Cherokee mother, with long coarse black hair, an adobe-colored complexion, and a smile that is as bright as her name, which means "sun." Selah—four years younger—helps out. Her name means "to pause," and she does so frequently, much to Shine's irritation.

This is a day of celebration, different from their usual Sunday dinners. Today, Dane Lightfoot, the Seminole member of the Trackers Team, is bringing a girlfriend. The doorbell sounds. Debby and Zorah—the identical twin girls—scream in unison, "He's here! He's here!"

Dane enters the doorway and calls for attention. "Everyone, I want you to meet someone. I want you to meet my fiancé. She's gorgeous, she's talented, and she's gifted. Lee, we should definitely train her. My wife will make a great Tracker," he announces as he ushers the woman into the room.

She is a year or two older than Shine, and she is breathtaking. Her name is Raven Looking Bird, and she is a Yavapai Indian. Her features are finely chiseled into unvarnished cherry wood skin; her small teeth are like perfectly matched pearls. Her glossy black hair is cut in a short bob, cropped at ear lobe level, with straight bangs to her eyebrows, and on her feet, she wears moccasins.

Seeing Lee sitting on the brick fireplace hearth, Noah Lightfoot—Dane's Creek Indian younger brother—walks over and takes a seat beside his mentor. They watch

Dane and Raven stroll hand in hand around the room talking to Wren, Graham, and each of the Thistleseed children. Lee smiles as he looks at them—his family—his friends—his team.

* * *

The Trackers Team was Lee's idea, formed out of a need to augment the efforts of local law enforcement to find criminals and missing persons. With the traditional methods hitting roadblocks at every turn, Lee offered his services as a clairvoyant to his friend, Chief Jack Abernathy. Though skeptical, Jack had seen the advantages of Lee's untraditional approach and enlisted his help on a few cases—behind closed doors, of course.

At the time, Lee's beacon—the person who brought his mind back to his body during the astral projection trips—was his friend and mentor, Jimbo Billie, a Seminole from the Lake Okeechobee area. Jimbo was older than Lee and did not travel, but he was skilled in mentally sending a signal light that only a clairvoyant could see. Growing weaker by the day from terminal pancreatic cancer, Jimbo had encouraged Lee to seek out and find others to train. The first one they chose was Dane Lightfoot.

Dane was a member of the Leon County Fire Department. He was fairly young—only eighteen—but a valuable member of their department. He seemed to be able to locate the source of a fire when even the arson inspector could not. He said he could "smell" it. That earned him the nickname "Bloodhound," which inevitably drew references to anything related to dogs. But it never seemed to bother Dane. He was good natured and laid back—traits he attributed to his Seminole Indian heritage and the fact that he was raised on a South Florida reservation.

Jimbo Billie had also lived on the reservation. Dane's father, Joe Lightfoot, had been a *Heles Pocase*—a Medicine Man. When Jimbo's parents and six older siblings were killed in a freak car accident, Joe Lightfoot "adopted" young Jimbo. Jimbo lived with the Lightfoots until Joe's wife died. Old Joe took a second wife shortly after that—a young beauty named Fawn, Jimbo's little sister, also spared in the accident and living with another family on the reservation.

Fawn gave birth to a son, and they named him Dane. According to Fawn, the name meant both "dweller in the valley" and "honorable." Dane was the seventh son of a seventh son. In their Indian beliefs, that meant he was destined to have the gift of second sight. Fawn insisted that he be given a name that insured he would be an honorable man if he was to possess power.

Jimbo had also been a seventh son and had manifested psychic gifts by the time he was twelve, so he knew well the accountability that came with power. When Dane was ten, Joe Lightfoot was killed by a rattlesnake that found its way into their *chickee* hut. According to the matrilineal Seminole tradition, boys were to be raised by the mother's family. As the natural uncle and adopted step-brother, that task fell to Jimbo Billie. He assumed the responsibility for Dane and Fawn, as well as the child that Fawn gave birth to nine months after Joe's death—Noah.

Lee Thistleseed's family lived in a neighboring town. Though he was Mohawk and not Seminole, he was allowed to visit the reservation for their social events. He and Jimbo met and became instant friends. Not only did they both have psychic gifts, they were also young men of integrity. They formed a partnership that included hours and hours of pushing each other to the limits of their clairvoyant abilities. They developed a method of tracking people, places, and things through an out-of-body experience called astral projection. Lee would send his mind on short, and then longer journeys, and Jimbo would concentrate on sending a signal light that brought Lee's mind back to his body. Thus, the Trackers Team began.

When Lee turned eighteen, he left South Florida and moved to Tallahassee to go to college. He and Jimbo kept in touch by mail and phone, and every couple of years they would "meet in the middle" to keep their tracking skills sharp. For 15 years, the two remained devoted friends and maintained their dream of forming a crime-fighting Trackers Team.

When Dane came of age, Lee—a tenured history professor at Florida State University—got him a job in Tallahassee at the fire department, and Jimbo moved north with his nephew. Before he left, Jimbo contacted a friend, who ran the Seminole Village and Culture Center in Tampa and arranged a job for Fawn in the *Coo-Taun Cho-Bee* or "where the big water meets the land" Museum. She and young Noah moved to Tampa to live in a *chickee* house that was reserved in the adjacent village for them.

Lee and Jimbo continued refining their skills and began working cases for the local police department. Six years later, when Jimbo was dying, they brought Dane on board and trained him as Jimbo's replacement. Dane's clairscent abilities were developed, and he left firefighting and joined the fire marshal's organization.

Jimbo Billie died just a year later, but not before he was able to lead Lee to Graham Skysong, a young Navajo singer who had a gift for clairaudience—psychic hearing. Graham was trained as the third member of the Trackers Team. When Noah was sixteen, he received an academic scholarship to F.S.U., and Lee helped him secure two privately funded grants. He moved to Tallahassee and bought a small "fixer-upper" house with the money from the grants. Shortly afterward, Noah also became a Tracker, bringing the team to its current four members.

* * *

Now, three years later, Lee is aware of the fidgeting young man beside him.

"How'd you do it?" Noah asks.

"How did I do what?" Lee asks.

"Bring her back. How'd you get Raven out of the

house before it blew?" He turns slightly to catch Lee's eye, but the older man remains motionless on the hearth, hands clasped loosely and elbows on his knees, watching the happy couple as they make their way around his family room and foyer.

"C'mon, Lee. I was there, remember? I saw John Silver Eyes carry Dane out of the burning house. He went back in for Raven, but he didn't come back out before it blew up. You couldn't carry her out. You were a hologram. Right?" Noah says.

"I was," he replies.

"So..." Noah says.

"So, I had to do something else," Lee says.

Frustration welling up in his chest, Noah stands and faces his friend. "What, man? What's the problem here? Why don't you just clear it up for me?"

Lee slowly reaches up and takes Noah's hand. "Sit down, Son. Let us not cause a scene. I would rather talk about it in a more private location, but as you are so insistent, I will explain what happened."

Noah resumes his place on the hearth, but he is taut as a piano wire. "You only made one backtrack in time, Lee. How did you get Raven out of Dane's house, and what's the deal with Jack Abernathy's kid?"

"Noah, did you ever read that science fiction story by Ray Bradbury titled *A Sound of Thunder?* It is about some men who went back in time to hunt a dinosaur."

"Oh, Lee. Please! Not with the stories again."

"Patience, Son. This is a short one. The men went back to the past to 'hunt' a Tyrannosaurus Rex that was already destined to be killed by a falling tree. They were instructed to stay on the path so as not to disturb the surroundings and cause catastrophic changes in the present. When the dinosaur appeared, one of the men became scared and stepped off the path. It was just one step, and he quickly righted himself, returning to the path without incident. It was not until he returned to the present that he realized the implications of his actions. Everything had changed—people, buildings, events, and even language was different. 'I only stepped off into the mud,' he said. But, alas. Looking at his shoe, he saw a tiny butterfly crushed in the sole. The death of that one creature had a ripple effect on time, and nothing was ever again the same."

"So, did you step on a butterfly?" Noah asks.

"Of sorts," Lee replies, "If you recall, our objective was to stop Darryl Kiley from finding a psychic Native American to use as an outlaw or a beacon. That was the only way we could keep him from using a tracker to tamper with the past to raise him to the political status he needed to become the next President."

"Did you kill him?" Noah asks, cocking his eyebrows up. "No. I scared him. He killed himself."

"Whoa! And…"

"And that was the butterfly. It set in motion the

events that bring us to here and now."

"Still lost, Buddy. Help me out."

Lee smiles indulgently. "Apparently, Darryl Kiley engineered the fire at Police Chief Abernathy's residence, and with Kiley gone, the house never burned..."

"...and four-year-old Andy Abernathy never died!"

"Exactly," Lee says, "ripple number one."

"Then Raven never revealed her automatic heiroscripting powers by painting the portrait of Mrs. Abernathy and the spirit of her son, Andy."

"Ripple number two. Keep going."

Noah's legs bounce up and down. He shifts sideways on the brick seat, eyes wide as he stares Lee in the face.

"So, you and Dane didn't go to her house to interview her and evaluate her psychic gift?"

"No. As far as anyone knows, today is the first time any of us have ever met Raven. That includes you, Noah. You have never met her. Do not forget that! See how the ripple grows? We cannot risk causing the butterfly effect."

"This is wild," Noah says. He slumps back against the fireplace, staring at the ceiling.

Noah's excitement is infectious, and Lee laughs at the boy's happiness, clapping him on the knee with his leathery hand. He glances at Dane and Raven talking with Shinehah. Graham is lurking nearby the couple, his eyes on the younger woman. *Good*, Lee thinks. *Graham and Shine will make a fine match.*

"Lee," Noah says, leaning forward again, "I'm still confused. What about the fire at Dane's house? What about my—my father, John Silver Eyes?"

"That fire still happened. I did not see it begin, so I can only speculate as to what really occurred. I believe Dane did, indeed, fall asleep on the sofa—by himself, this time. But judging from the fact that Dane has just come from Andy's baptism at the Mormon church, I am fairly certain that he did not drink any wine, so he was not as impaired as he was when the event took place two years ago as you and I—and only you and I—remember it."

"O.K. I get that. Another ripple. How'd the fire start?"

"Not Raven's cigarette, this time. Your—um—the Outlaw, I suppose. But Dane was able to get to safety before the fire completely consumed his house."

"Makes sense. What about the Outlaw? He was still there outside, waiting to kill Dane, wasn't he? I saw him—spoke to him when I backtracked to that night," Noah says.

For the first time, Lee shows some discomfort. *How do I tell him what I did—how I lured his father into the house to die?* He looks long and hard at the boy he loves like his own son, and then he does something he has never done before. He lies to him.

"I do not know, Noah. We will have to find out from Dane," Lee says avoiding Noah's eager gaze. "He is, after all, a deputy fire marshal, and I am sure he tracked the arson's origin."

Noah stares at the floor for a long time before he speaks again. "If John Silver Eyes is still alive, we'll have to..."

"No. We will not. If John Silver Eyes is still alive, we will find him and keep track of his activities, so he can never backtrack again," Lee says emphatically.

"What about my mother?" Noah asks.

Lee's heart constricts to see the agony in the young man's eyes. He gently places his hand on Noah's shoulder. "Your mother will never be bothered by him again, Noah. I promise."

"Hey, Hona! Why so serious?" Dane says.

Lee and Noah jump up, startled that Dane has gotten so close to them during this touchy conversation. They are keenly aware of the importance of shielding Dane from this business. *The worst part of keeping a secret is not telling those you love.* Noah Lightfoot and Liahona Thistleseed are the only persons in the world who know of the science fiction story that has played out in the past few days, and that's the way it must stay. *No more ripples*, Lee decides.

"I think it is very serious that you have kept this beautiful lady from us," Lee says. He grins and claps Dane on the back. Snaking an arm around Raven, he gives her a fatherly kiss on the cheek, and then saunters toward the kitchen to mingle with the rest of his family.

"Hona, wait up," calls Dane. Turning to Noah, he grins. "Take care of my woman for a few minutes, little bro. I've got to talk to Lee. Back in a bit, Babe." He leans over and nuzzles Raven, and then hurries after Lee, leaving Noah alone to "get acquainted" with his future sister-in-law.

Raven stands eye to eye with Noah. She is close enough for him to catch a whiff of her signature vanilla-scented perfume, *DeVanille*. He knows it well; indeed, he knows her well. In another reality, just a few days earlier, he was her friend and—almost—her lover. His gut cramps from the memory.

She smiles brilliantly. "Well, Noah. I guess we'll soon be seeing a lot of each other."

"Yeah. Guess so." His attempt at being nonchalant falls short. His hands tremble.

Sensing his nervousness, she makes small talk. "Dane says you're a freshman at F.S.U., and you're 'Chief Osceola' for the football games."

"Go 'Noles' and all that," he says, nodding.

"That's pretty exciting, I bet. What's your major?"

"At this point, I'm just majoring in Renegade, the mascot horse." He laughs slightly.

"What's your gift?" she asks.

Startled at the bluntness of her question, he just stares at her with his mouth hanging open.

"Come on," she says, "Dane's explained all about the team and how you all have one or more psychic gifts. So what's yours?"

"Um, it's remote viewing—seeing things that happen far away from where I am. Lee's a remote viewer, too, but his powers manifest differently. I've also got a photographic memory."

"Now that's really neat. How's that work?"

Staring directly into her face, he can't help but show off. "You came in behind Dane. He reached around your back and nudged you forward. Your moccasin caught on the edge of the threshold for an instant, and you looked down to make sure you weren't going to trip. Dane's hand slid to your waist. You reached up and pushed at your bangs, poking your hair behind your ears, and then shook it loose. You bit down on your lower lip, licked at the corner of your mouth, clenched your right fist, and then smiled. Want me to go on?"

Her mouth comes open while he talks. It hangs slack for a moment, and then she lifts the corners into the most radiant smile he has ever seen. It reaches all the way to the corners of her sienna-colored eyes. "You are the bomb!" she exclaims.

"That I am," he confirms. "You look a little thirsty, almost-sister. Let's get you a Diet Coke from the fridge."

Her smile falters a bit. "How'd you know I like to drink Diet Coke?"

"I must be psychic!" He winks, and then leads her through the crowded family room.

On the way to the kitchen, they notice Dane and Lee

outside on the patio, locked in what looks to be a serious conversation. Dane is pacing and pinching the bridge of his nose, something he does when he detects a smell. He is a clairscent, with psychic sensitivities centered around a heightened sense of smell, and the odors he picked up in the wee hours of the morning have resurfaced. He cocks his head from side to side as if searching for the origin.

"It was a weird smell, Lee. Fruity and floral mixed with pungent and nasty. I even tasted it! Yech. Couldn't get enough water to drink afterwards," he says.

"When we finish dinner, we'll try to get away and track it," Lee says.

"Gotta be later on. I've got plans with Raven, if you know what I mean."

"Indeed," Lee says, pulling his mouth up in his well-known half grin.

"Mind in the gutter, Hona! Not what you think. I'm evaluating her psychic gifts, not her physical ones. She looks to be a type of automatic writer, only she manifests with pictures instead of text. Pretty cool, if you ask me. She'll be a tremendous asset to the team."

"I have no doubt. Is she amenable to training?"

"She says she is. I want you to do it, though. I'm too close to be objective."

"I will be happy to train her. It will be my honor." Lee opens the patio door and steps into the breakfast room.

"Good deal, then." Dane twitches his nose and sniffs

the air deeply.

"The scent again?" Lee's eyebrow lifts as he turns to look at Dane.

"Yeah. It's really strong, too." He takes another deep breath, holds it, and then he exhales. "Yep. That's exactly what I thought. Pot roast!"

Coming up behind Lee, Wren pokes him in the side. "Pot roast, it is. And it's ready to be served. Shop talk later. Come on to the dining room, and grab your sweetheart, Dane, before your brother charms her away from you. I don't know about you, but I'm hungry. Let's all get ready to eat." She hugs him fiercely before exiting the kitchen.

In the dining room, Dane catches Raven's eye and moves over to where she and Noah are standing. Lee and Wren move to opposite ends of the large dining table. Graham, Shine, and Cyrus—the oldest son—are to their right, Raven and the Lightfoot brothers assemble on the left. The six other Thistleseed children gather in the doorway between the dining room and the foyer. The room is full of friends and family and much love. Lee takes Wren's hand in his and signals for the children to begin the blessing song from the LDS Primary Song Book that always precedes their meals.

Shine and the five girls begin.

"Thank you, dear Lord, for the things we may need,
So we may serve you in word and by deed,
Let us be faithful in work and in play,

Thank you, Father, for blessings this day.

Lee and Wren sing the second verse.

"Thank you, dear Lord, for the wisdom and might
To teach our children to choose what is right,
Let us be role models—husbands and wives
Thank you, Father, for blessing our lives"

The three boys—no slackers in the vocal department— finish the song with the last verse.

"Thank you, dear Lord, for our good daily bread.
We know that it is by Your hand we're fed.
Let us be humble and show gratitude.
Thank you, Father, for blessing our food."

At the end of the song, the family and all the guests say, "Amen." The six younger Thistleseeds retire to the card tables in the family room set up especially for them, with Bill and Selah acting as the "adult" table heads. The "over 21" adults sit down at the huge dining room table. In minutes, the entire household can be heard eating and praising Wren's outstanding Southern feast: fork tender pot roast basted in its own juices for hours in the oven, mashed Yukon potatoes whipped with sweet cream butter and sour cream, brown gravy made with a roux from the pot roast juices, fresh field peas and green bean snaps flavored with bacon drippings, buttered corn on the cob, fluffy cat head biscuits, and juicy peach cobbler with heavy cream.

CHAPTER TWO
SCENTS OF LOSS

PROPPED UP AGAINST THE PILLOWS on Dane's bed and still full from eating dinner, Raven yawns for the fourth time. She stretches her arms over her head and rolls to her stomach, lifts up on her elbows, and puts her chin in her hands. Dane stands at the mirror brushing his long black hair. She smiles at the irony this simple act brings. *What a gender reversal we are—long-haired man; short-haired woman.* A slight giggle escapes her lips.

    Dane turns to look at her. "What?" he asks.

    "Nothing," she says, "just watching you."

    "Am I that entertaining?"

"Sometimes."

    He puts down the brush and hops onto the bed with her. "So, what did you think of my extended family?" he asks.

    "They're great. I love the way all those kids help

each other out."

"That's how it is in a big family. I call it 'the trickle-down' method of child-rearing."

"Explain, please," she says, rolling to her back with her hands behind her head. She kicks off her moccasins, rubs her feet together and flexes her toes. She yawns again.

"The 'trickle-down' method—as invented by Mr. Dane Lightfoot. Listen carefully, and learn, my dear. Cy and Shine Thistleseed were the firstborn twins. They were the guinea pigs. They got all the brand-new clothes, wore the cloth diapers, and received the closest supervision. Four years later, here come Bill and Selah. Fortunately, they were the second set of boy/girl twins. The clothing trickled down to them, they wore clean—albeit secondhand—diapers, and they had a little less supervision. After all, now Lee and Wren have four children under the age of five."

"Go on," Raven says.

"Another four years pass, and Lee hangs his pants on the headboard again."

"What's that mean?"

"They joke that every time Lee hangs his pants on the headboard, Wren gets pregnant."

Raven laughs, with an unpretentious Julia Roberts "Pretty Woman" kind of joy. Dane's heart jumps in his chest. *Thank you, God, for this woman!*

"Anyway," he continues, "Wren hits another double, but this time—two girls. Debby and Zorah emerge on the scene, and things get really interesting. Trickle down the clothing, but make some adjustments to the boy stuff, you know. Forget the cloth diapers. Now it's time for the disposable ones. And as for supervision, well, some of that trickled down to Cy and Shine from the folks. You need help when you have six kids! But then, four more years later, Wren finally gets a single. Kenny is the *man*. And by that, I mean he's the seventh son of the seventh son—destined to be the one with second sight like his dad. So, he gets the trickled down boy clothing—minus adjustments—*plus* the girl stuff—with adjustments, of course. Supervision falls to Cy, Shine, Bill, and Selah 'cause Wren's really got her hands full now. But it's all good. And they just keep on trickling down from the oldest to the youngest. Not a bad system, if you ask me. And then, just when it seems that the Thistleseed household is finished with babies—surprise! Shelly arrives, and *everything* trickles down to her! Pretty neat theory, huh?"

Dane looks at Raven for confirmation of his genius, and she snores—sound asleep. He folds half the bedspread over her legs, kisses her forehead, and goes into the living room, quietly shutting the bedroom door behind him. Plopping down on the couch, he flicks on the television to catch whatever team is happening to play football this afternoon. After a few minutes, his eyes close, and he is also snoring.

* * *

The woman studied herself in the mirror. Her hair was perfectly styled and highlighted, her makeup impeccable, her eyes much, much too dilated. She tilted her head first to one side, then the other. On her dressing table was a vast array of beauty products, expensive satin-lined cases, and crystal bottles. She reached forward and touched the shiny crystal containers that held her perfumes. They sparkled like diamonds, sending off showers of colors that she didn't know existed. She pursed her glossed lips in an "oo" shape, approving of the high color in her cheeks and across her forehead.

For a moment, she looked confused. A tall glass of red wine beckoned her, and she drained it in four swallows before refilling it from the adjacent decanter. She drained that glass just as quickly, and then refilled her glass again. Delicately touching her tongue to each side of her mouth, she studied her lipstick, pleased that there was no smudging.

She shifted her position on the silk-covered stool and was surprised to hear a tinkling sound. At her feet she observed no less than three empty wine bottles. *Curious, but they do make such a lovely sound.* She nudged them against each other again, giggling at the pretty music they made, and then slipped the alpaca cardigan off her shoulders, letting it lie where it fell beside her stool.

The rainbow lights on the table caught her attention again. She selected a lavender globe-shaped *Lavande* bottle with a jeweled bulb—her most recent favorite. Looking in the mirror, she watched herself grip the bulb and squeeze. The fine mist of fragrance hovered in front of the atomizer in slow motion. She was fascinated with the journey the droplets made from the bottle to her neck. She inhaled deeply, and some of the mist entered her airway, coating her tongue with a bitterness she found unpleasant, so she drank from the wine glass again. *Better—much, much better,* she thought dreamily. She dropped the wine glass onto the floor. *Oops!*

She squeezed the bulb again, and again, and again, until her hair was damp, and her makeup ran in rivulets down her cheeks. The crystal perfume bottle fell from her grip and broke when it contacted the pile of wine bottles at her feet. *Pretty music,* she thought. She drank directly from the Baccarat decanter until it was empty, then she tipped it over the edge of the table. She clapped her hands at the sound.

Reaching forward, she pulled all the perfume and makeup bottles off the table and let them crash to the floor. The cacophony of sound made her laugh so hard she slipped off the stool, landing on her back atop the shards. Her bare back was deeply lacerated from shoulders to hips, perfume seeping into the wounds. The delicate fragrances combined into a mélange of odors mingled with the coppery aroma of blood. *I don't like this smell.* She moaned. *I don't like this. I don't...like...* She whimpered, and then she was still.

* * *

"Dane!" Raven shouts, standing over her moaning

fiancé on the couch. His eyes are closed tightly, and his hands are clamped over his nose.

"I...don't...like...this...smell," he says.

She kneels at his head and pats his shoulder. "Wake up, honey. Wake up."

He twitches violently. Raven gently pulls his hands from his nose. He takes a breath and cries out as the malodorous scent fills his sinuses. He pushes his fists against his eye sockets, moaning and rolling face first to the floor. He crawls a few feet, panting like a dog, Raven knee-walking behind him.

"Dane. What's wrong? Is it a dream? A vision? What do I do?" She is frantic.

"Hona," he gasps. "Please...call...call...Hona. Ohh! I...need...a...light. Oh, my guuungh."

Raven snatches the phone from its cradle and begins punching in the number for the Thistleseed house. Selah answers on the third ring.

"Get your dad! Your dad! Something's wrong with Dane. Hurry, please!" Raven cries. In the background, she can hear Selah screaming for her father, then heavy footfalls as Lee Thistleseed runs to the phone.

"Raven. Is he conscious?" Lee asks.

"Yes, but he's—No, I don't know. He said to call you. Please, please help him."

"Keep him talking. Don't let him drift off to sleep. I'll be right there," Lee says, and then he turns and shouts to

Wren, who is now at the doorway. "Call Noah! Call him now, little bird. Send him to Dane's."

Lee runs to his car without bothering to put on shoes. He knows what has happened. Dane picked up a scent track without a beacon present, and that's one of the most dangerous things that a Tracker can ever do. It will take both he and Noah to bring Dane back to himself. Timing is critical, so Lee speeds through the streets, hoping to avoid traffic cops. He does not intend to lose Dane again.

As Lee pulls into Dane's driveway, Noah screeches to a halt behind him and jumps out of the red mustang. They don't speak; they don't knock. They burst into the house and find Dane keening on the floor with Raven stroking his hair, rapidly murmuring into his ear.

"Do it, do it," Lee says to Noah.

They both drop to the floor. Lee pushes Raven out of the way and wraps his arms around Dane. Noah slides up against the couch, closes his eyes, and is soon breathing deeply. Lee rocks Dane like a mother holding her child, cooing softly and looking intently at Noah to make sure the young man is in his trance. In Lee's iron embrace, Dane moans, slowly moving his head from side to side. Wet spots appear at Lee's eyes and beneath his nose. *Please, please, God. Let us be in time.*

Dane's movements slow down, and he relaxes, slumping lower to the floor. A few moments later he takes a deep breath, and then lets it out in a shuddering stream. In a voice that is just barely audible, Dane speaks one short little word, "Home," and then he lies still.

"Is he...is he dead?" Raven says. Tears stream from her wide eyes.

"No, he's just sleeping now," Noah says. "He'll be O.K.— just needs rest."

Lee loosens his hold on the sleeping man, grabs a pillow from the sofa, and puts it beneath Dane's head. Reaching into a nearby basket, he pulls a chenille afghan out and covers him. Rising, his knees make popping sounds that draw Noah's attention. Lee shrugs.

The two men sit on the couch, but Raven stays on the floor at Dane's side.

"What happened?" she asks.

"Raven, I hate that you witnessed this, but in a way, it's good that you did. Your training will include ways to avoid 'getting lost' like Dane did today," Lee says.

"Getting lost?"

"Yeah. That's what happens when you track by yourself. Your mind gets lost in darkness while your body is left behind. The first rule of tracking—never track without a beacon," Noah says. "Lee has the mortality margin fixed at 50 minutes."

"I'm sorry. I really don't understand the beacon part and the mortality margin. What do you mean?" she says.

"The most important person in a psychic track is the beacon," Lee says. "Your beacon is the silver cord that keeps your mind and body connected. When you are journeying in your mind, you must have a lighthouse—a beacon—to get you home, or you will die."

Raven pales visibly. "Die?"

"Uh huh. And that's why you heard Dane say the word 'home' just before he relaxed. He was asking me to bring him home," Noah says.

"But surely Dane knows that. Why would he do such a dangerous thing?" Raven asks.

"Dane is unique," Lee says. "Sometimes the scents find him before he can search for them. It leaves him very vulnerable to exactly what you saw today. He carries a pager in his pocket for these occurrences. We all do."

At that moment, they hear a rhythmic high-pitched sound coming from the bedroom. Noah holds his own pager in the air.

"I think I found his beeper," he says, looking at Raven.

She blushes slightly but offers no explanation.

Lee leans forward. "Raven," he says, "if you love him as you seem to, it is imperative that you safeguard him. You will be his lifeline. I am sorry to put such responsibility on you, but you will be with Dane more than any of the rest of us. Can I count on you?"

Raven looks at him unwaveringly. "I will never, ever allow anything to happen to Dane."

"Good deal! I'll let you marry him, then." Noah says,

laughing at Raven's expression.

Lee shakes his head and rolls his eyes. *How I love these boys*, he thinks. Getting to his feet, he pats Dane carefully on the back, and then heads for the door. Noah follows him.

"Hey, wait. What do I do now?" Raven asks.

"Watch T.V. He'll be out for a while," Noah says. "And when he wakes up, he's gonna be really hungry. If you can't cook—and I know that you can't—better order *Domino's Pizza*."

Where are you going?" Raven asks.

Noah yawns. "Home to finish my nap. These two o'clock meals really do me in."

"What did you say?" she asks, but the door is already closing. *Weird. I swear I've heard him say that before. This Déjà vu is starting to get to me.* Then, taking a place on the couch, she turns up the volume to cover the sound of the snoring from the floor and scans the phone book for the pizza delivery number.

CHAPTER THREE
TRAINING

"No, Raven. The word you use to call your beacon is 'home.' You do not say, 'get me outta here' followed by an expletive," Lee says.

On the couch, Noah, Graham, and Dane convulse with laughter. Raven glares at them, and they shut up—briefly. She twists her mouth into a scowl as she scans the scribbled paper in front of her. Putting down her pencil, she leans back and sighs.

"This is not as easy as I thought it would be," she says.

"Nobody said it would be easy, but I have faith in you, Babe," Dane says. "Just remember—the word is not..."

"BLEEP," the couch brigade says in unison.

The room erupts in a fresh round of laughter, including Lee who has tried valiantly up to this point to remain objective and neutral. Raven balls up the paper and hurls it at the couch, and then she gives up and joins in the frivolity. After a few minutes of playful teasing, Lee stands and stretches, drains his glass of ice tea, and addresses the young men.

"Alright, gentlemen. We have had enough of fun time. Which of you can be serious enough to beacon this time?"

"I'm good to go," Graham says. "I only laughed a little." His eyes behind the wire-rimmed glasses look innocent, but his tightly pressed mouth gives him away.

Lee surveys the assemblage of male Trackers. "Noah," he says. "You stay. Dane and Graham. You two take a ride to town and bring us back some lunch." When nobody moves, Lee adds heavily, "My treat."

That sets them all in motion. Noah takes his place at the table. Dane takes the money Lee offers. *Typical.* Graham grabs his jacket and saunters out the door to get the car. The wind catches the door and blows it open wider, filling the room with a decidedly chilly feeling for the first week of October. Lee shivers, catching the door to keep it from hitting the wall. *It is going to be a cold winter*, he observes. And for some reason, it bothers him. He looks back to see Raven gathering the afghan from the basket. She wraps it around her shoulders and returns to her seat. Noah watches her with unguarded eyes. *He is remembering his time with her.* Lee frowns slightly. *We will have to talk about this later—alone, and someday, I will have to tell him about his father's death.* He shakes the dread away and puts a smile on his face.

"Alright, you two. Shall we begin again?" Lee says.

Raven tilts her head back and stares at the ceiling, dropping her jaw and sticking out her tongue. "Bleah! Let's do it. I don't know why this is so hard for me, Lee."

Lee sympathizes with her and gives her some more pointers. "It has only been three days, Raven. Training takes a while. You have done well so far."

"I'm doing terrible! I can draw so much better than this. Really, I can."

Noah laughs at her frustration. This is quite different from the confident young woman he brings to mind from just several days ago. *Back then, she was on equal, if not better, footing with the rest of us. Her sketches were spot on, with details so minute they had to be enlarged with a makeshift magnifier made from a juice glass. And her beaconing powers were...* He stops, and his eidetic memory kicks in, and he remembers. *Her beaconing powers were so good they were used against the team by the Outlaw, John Silver Eyes.*

* * *

Noah had just regained consciousness after being drugged with ether. He struggled to orient himself—to recall where he was and what he had been doing. He remembered. He had been in the middle of beaconing for Lee's track when it happened. Lee was backtracking to find Darryl Kiley, the man who was using a Native American tracker to boost himself to Presidential candidacy. *No, not to find him—to kill him.* Suddenly he had lost contact with Lee. *Lee!* Noah realized he left him tracking alone, without a beacon. In 50 minutes, Lee would die, if he was not dead already. Noah knew where he was now. He was in the Outlaw's house. The Outlaw was John Silver, Governor Kiley's associate—*personal thug was more like it.* The man had been watching him. When Noah came to the first time—after the guy coldcocked him—and tried to attack the man, he was put out again with the ether. His head was pounding, but he knew he would have to send a beacon signal without the Outlaw noticing. Noah closed his eyes and prepared to give the signal.

The sound of the doorbell renewed the ache in his head, but it also gave him the opportunity to beacon for Lee without being detected by the Outlaw. He heard the man arguing with someone. The Beacon. Noah knew the voice. It was Raven, and it broke his heart. He sent the signal, hoping Lee would find it and come home.

Raven rushed over and sat beside Noah. He feigned unconsciousness, drawing on all his reserves not to move away from her. He was so angry. *Why would she do this?* She had been a member of the Trackers Team for three years—since before Dane was killed in the house fire. He remained very still and listened to the heated conversation she had with the Outlaw.

"If you harm him, I will kill you, John Silver," she

snarled, her eyes narrowed to slits.

"Harm him? Never. He is my son," the Outlaw said. His nostrils flared as he met her glare.

The word evoked confusion in Noah. *Son?*

"Noah is my son—my seventh son, to be precise. Twenty years ago, I fell in love with his mother and seduced her. She spurned me because of a dream. She said she was told to take my son and raise him as a Seminole..." Silver Eyes said.

What? I'm NOT a Seminole? Noah wondered.

"...and that dream robbed me of my gifted son and his irreplaceable mother. I will track back and enter Fawn's dream and give her instructions to marry me instead," Silver Eyes said.

"Then you would become his father," Raven said.

"I AM his father," he said.

My father? This man is my father? The Outlaw? Noah moaned, barely audible.

"What about Dane?" Raven asked.

The Outlaw spat air. "Bah, why waste your heart on Dane when Noah is the superior man? As the son of an up-and-coming political genius, he will have tremendous wealth and power. However, if you have no interest, I can arrange it so Noah will despise you..."

As if I ever would or even could, Noah thought with a pain in his heart.

"No. Take your trip. I don't wish to lose Noah like I

lost Dane," Raven said.

Noah's heart broke as he put the pieces together—Raven and Dane, his mother and John Silver Eyes. Thereafter, the events occurred rather quickly. The Outlaw prepared to backtrack, and Raven used Noah's own Bowie knife to stab the man, killing him instantly. She cut Noah's bindings and put the knife in his hand, and then rolled the body of his father next to him to make it look like Noah had killed the man. Before she left, she whispered in his ear. Noah remembered the smell of her cologne mixed with the metallic odor of blood and death, and it repulsed him.

"Oh, Noah," she said. "You are so much like them both. Thank goodness you will never be as your father. But, sadly, you can never be your brother, either."

After that, he had called the police. When Jack Abernathy arrived, he did not recognize Noah because his memory had been erased from one of the Outlaw's earlier backtracks. Governor Kiley had been there, too, after hearing his associate's address over the police scanner. Kiley had bribed Abernathy to let Noah go, calling the death an accident—insinuating that Mr. Silver tripped and fell on a large kitchen knife. *Sure. That oughta fly.* But, evidently, Jack bought it because Noah was released without even having to be questioned at police headquarters.

Noah's first order of business was to make sure Lee had found the tracking beacon. With that assurance, he next visited Maria Ramirez. *Oooh. Don't have the energy to think about Maria right now.* Noah winced, the ache in his heart yet fresh from the thought of her. Then he summoned up the next thing that happened in the sequence of events. He confronted Raven at her apartment. She told him that the Outlaw had her on a short leash after threatening to harm her mother in Arizona. She also told him that John Silver Eyes was a shape shifter who could appear as a hologram in the past, and he used that ability to lure people into dangerous situations.

"He killed Dane?" Noah asked.

"No. I killed Dane," Raven said. "I caused the fire that killed Dane. We had dinner, and I brought some wine. Dane didn't want any, but I insisted. You knew Dane quit smoking?"

"I guess so. That's why I was surprised he fell asleep smoking," Noah said.

"He didn't. I did. We were sitting on the couch discussing wedding plans. The wine made us sleepy, and I was smoking. My cigarette touched off the rug. The next thing I knew, I was outside on the ground—safe, and Dane was inside the house—burning," she said.

Raven told him how and why John Silver Eyes had been at the house to kill Dane.

"When Dane was ten, just a little boy, he saw a man put a rattlesnake beneath a blanket in his father's *chickee.* The man had silver eyes. When his father returned to the hut, the rattlesnake struck him. Dane saw his father die. He said

John Silver Eyes gave him 'the evil eye.' Dane realized the man he interviewed almost twenty years later was the same man that killed his father, and he was sure the man remembered him, too."

Funny how things get so mixed up, Noah observed. When he backtracked to Dane's house later that evening, he ended up at that very time she spoke of. He saw John Silver outside Dane's house, watching as the fire threatened to burn the two people inside. Seeing Noah, the man had begun chanting in the Muskogee language to ward him off, as if he were an evil spirit.

"John Silver Eyes. Save them. You have to get them out or they'll die," Noah said.

The man continued to chant, backing away from Noah, clutching at the bushes in fear.

"Get them out. Please. Father. Do it for me. Let me remember you as someone who once had love in his heart—for my mother—for me—for your son," Noah begged.

Noah watched the man as John rushed into the burning building and returned, carrying Dane over his shoulder. When he went back in to save Raven, the house exploded. Noah would never forget the way his father looked at him just before he entered the house.

"Noah?" John Silver Eyes said.

* * *

"Noah?" Lee says. He places his hand on Noah's shoulder and shakes him slightly.

"Earth to Noah," Raven says, meaning to make a joke, but uncomfortable all the same.

Noah's eyes are misted over from dredging up those memories. Aware that his friends are watching him, he gives an exaggerated yawn and rubs his eyes.

"Well, are we gonna do this thing or not?" he asks.

"Where were you?" asks Raven.

"I was in the land of boredom," Noah yawns. "Food here yet? I'm starving."

"Welcome back. We have missed you," Lee says sardonically. "And, no. The food has not arrived. Be patient."

"It's drive-through. They should be back by now. I'm starving," Noah says.

Always starving, Lee observes. "I have an idea. Let us change things up a bit. Noah, you can track, and we can work on Raven's beaconing skills…" Lee begins.

"NO!" Noah shouts. "Let's don't. I—um—I've got to see a man about a dog first."

"What dog?" Raven asks.

Lee shakes his head, drawing the corners of his mouth down sharply.

"Sorry," Noah whispers as he gets up quickly from the chair. He shrugs his shoulders and leans in a little closer to her. "That means I've got to pee." He tiptoes out of the room.

Raven opens her mouth to comment, but really has nothing to say. Fortunately, mere moments later, the door swings open. Dane and Graham enter, holding a huge bucket of Kentucky Fried Chicken.

"Braaaackk, pluck, pluck, pluck, pluck," Graham clucks. "Dinner is served."

They clear off the table and set the bucket in the center, laying out napkins to serve as plates. Noah returns from the bathroom and grabs a drumstick, cramming it into his mouth.

"Stop!" Dane says. "Bless it first, little bro."

Noah withdraws a partially denuded chicken leg. Bowing his head and looking properly chastised, he looks at the others, waiting for them to bow their heads, too.

"Bless the food on this table...and all that is within. Amen," he says through a mouthful of chicken. Then, laughing, he polishes off the remainder of the leg and reaches in for more.

"So, how'd it go this time?" Dane asks.

"We didn't get anything done. Your little brother had to 'see a man about a dog' first," Raven says.

Chicken spews from several mouths at once as all the men—including Lee—laugh.

Noah lifts his hands in resignation. "A man's gotta do what a man's gotta do."

"That may be, but a man does not need to tell a lady about it," Lee says.

"I'm sorry, Hona. The boy's got no couth. What can I say?" Dane says. He nudges Raven in the side. "Now what were you saying about how you liked my family?"

"I love your family. I do. I really do," she says. "I can't wait to meet your mother."

"She's a keeper. Hey, Noah. When's the last time you saw Mom?" Dane says.

"Before school started. I dunno. Like two months, maybe. It was back in the summer, just after Hurricane Andrew hit down south. I tried to get Mom to leave, but she wouldn't budge from the village."

"That's Mom. Good thing we didn't inherit that stubborn gene of hers."

"Oh, that's for sure. Like it's not the main substance in our blood, bro."

This draws laughter from all the rest in the room. It's a well-known fact that the Lightfoot boys are the epitome of mule-headed stubbornness.

"We're going down in a few days. Want to come along?"

"Can't. Got football games, you know, every weekend. When's the wedding planned, by the way?"

Raven and Dane exchange looks. "We were thinking around Thanksgiving," she says.

More spewed chicken. Noah wipes his mouth, figuring up the time frame. "Wow. Short engagement. Well, O.K. Can you do me a favor, though. Don't have it on a Saturday. I really don't want to be the best man in my Chief Osceola getup."

"Who said you were the best man?" Dane quips, receiving a shocked look from his bother. "Nah, don't worry. You will always be my best man, little bro."

"O.K. I've had enough. Who's going to bleep for me?" Raven asks.

"I seem to be the only one not still wolfing down the Colonel's finest finger-lickin' chicken, so I will beacon again for you," Lee says smiling. "Men, please try to eat quietly."

Graham and Dane move back to the couch. Noah grabs the bucket of chicken and squeezes in beside them. Though the atmosphere is jovial, they know better than to interrupt a track. All three of them will be sitting on the ready in case something goes wrong. They are the sentries—the watchdogs. Any one of them will jump in and beacon at the slightest hint of trouble. They continue eating, all the while keeping an eye on Lee and Raven as she begins her track.

Her breathing slows, and her chest makes the steady rise and fall they know so well as the body giving way to the mind. Behind her eyelids, the jerky REM movements are very apparent. She takes one short intake of breath, and then her hand starts moving on the table. Clutching a pencil between her fingers, she rapidly sketches on a large piece of blank paper. The three men on the couch lean forward, mesmerized with the phenomenon of automatic writing—a gift none of them possesses. Her movements are hesitant at first, and then grow more confident.

This time, she's gonna do it! Noah thinks. He is

anxious to see what she draws.

Raven's hand moves like a scampering mouse over the paper. She outlines, she adds shading, she stabs at the paper with the point, wearing the pencil down to the wood. Even when the point is completely gone, she continues. Dane quickly, but carefully, pulls the pencil from her grasp and pushes a sharpened one between her fingers. Her hand seems to have its own mind as it travels around the paper. She draws in the middle and all around the sides, the images overlapping, moving from one scene to another, covering the paper completely with graphite.

Suddenly, she stiffens. Her hand clenches around the pencil, and it snaps in half with a loud cracking sound.

"Get me, get me, HOME!" Raven hollers, causing all the seated men to jump back. Her eyes fly open, and she looks wildly around the room. "Yeooooww!" she cries out. "In my back. Get it out! Get it out now!"

Dane leaps off the couch and grabs her shoulders, raising her t-shirt to look at her back. Seeing nothing there, he looks quizzically at the others and shrugs his shoulders.

"Babe...?" he says to her. But Raven pulls away from him and is staring at the drawing.

"Raven?" Lee says. "Are you alright?"

"I did this? I did this! Look. Look at it! I drew this. I saw it. I did!" Raven says.

She laughs like a child, holding the paper up for all to see as if it is a first-place ribbon.

Noah and Graham clap their hands, applauding her first successful track. Raven drops the paper on the table and dances around the room doing a stereotypical war dance, complete with "whoop, whoop, whoop" sound effects and palm to the mouth, much to the entertainment of her audience.

Lee spreads the paper out on the table to study. Dane joins him, still laughing at his adorable fiancé hopping in place.

The paper is a mass of images from various points of view. A table, a mirrored image of a woman with black streaks below her eyes, a hand holding a goblet. Bottles of different shapes and sizes dominate the drawing. Some are upright, but others are on their sides, with liquid spilling from them. More are broken, shattered, piled up on the floor. One large bottle fills the center of the page. The word *Lavande* is etched into the base of the bottle. It is globe-shaped with a jeweled bulb atomizer, and a fine mist fans out from its tip.

"Oh, dear God," Dane whispers, just before his knees buckle.

CHAPTER FOUR
AGONY AND ESCSTACY

"KEEP LOOKING, JACK," LEE SAYS into the phone as he paces in a tight circle. "She would have been roughly in her late-thirties or early-forties. Blonde. Found amid a pile of broken wine bottles, perfumes, and cosmetics." He listens for a moment. "Yes. Dane scented her yesterday. One of our team has drawn the scene." Another moment. "Yes. That is correct. We have an artist now. Will you call me immediately if you find something? Thank you."

Raven's mood is decidedly subdued from her earlier excitement. She did, indeed, draw a crime scene, but she failed to realize at the time that the scene was one of death. Dane sits with his arm around her, squeezing her shoulder. At the table, Noah and Graham examine the drawing, hoping to find more clues about the incident and the woman involved.

"Jack will notify us should he discover anything, but he seems pretty sure that nothing of this nature has happened here," Lee says. His pacing slows, and the circle widens.

"Say it," Noah prompts.

Lee stops with his back to them. He turns slowly and regards the young man.

"O.K., I'll say it," Noah says. "She's not anywhere around here. So, let's find her. I'll go see what I can see."

"I'll light," Graham says.

Sitting in chairs opposite each other with their arms resting on the small maple table top, Noah and Graham close their eyes and begin breathing slowly and deeply in sync. They make no other movements and would seem to the uninformed observer to be napping. Raven is rapt with attention. Her eyes flick from one to the other. Dane nudges her, and she sucks in a quick mouthful of air, surprised to realize she has been holding her breath. She takes his hand and squeezes it while she stares at the Trackers before her.

Noah is the first to move. His jaw twitches ever so slightly as he whispers the word, "Home." Then he opens his eyes. Less than a second later, Graham opens his own eyes, and they stare at one another. Noah grins and winks, making Graham break into a smile. Noah rotates his shoulders and becomes serious. Looking at a spot somewhere over Graham's left shoulder, he begins to relate his journey.

"It's her bedroom. Walls are painted mauve with white crown molding, white baseboards. Curtains are brocade with gold braided tie-backs. Immaculate. Could pass the white glove test. Except for that dressing table. What a mess. Furniture is glossy white French Provincial with pink inserts and gold handles. The stool is covered with silk, but it's stained with a red liquid. Not blood. I'm guessing red wine from the looks of the bottles on the floor.

There are at least three empties there, along with a bunch of perfume bottles—most of them broken, shattered. It looks like someone just swept everything off the table. Black smudges on the table top. Police dusted for fingerprints. Dusted the bottles, too. Blood on the glass all over the carpet. That must have been extremely painful, judging from the amount of blood and the large area covered by the stains. Doesn't look like a homicide, though. No struggle—just a mass of broken stuff around that table area.

Can't tell how she died, unless she bled out from cuts inflicted by the glass shards. She must have just laid there, bleeding."

"Did you see anything written? Mail, diary, receipt?" Graham asks.

Noah cocks his head to the side and stares again at the wall. "I see that bottle with the word *Lavande* etched in it. Bunches of labels on the perfumes. *Diamant, Épice d'Asie, Eau de something, Chatoyant No. 2.* Wait. There is a little piece of paper on the floor near the wastebasket. Yes! A credit card receipt. And there's her name. It's—M-a-r..."

"Mary?" Dane asks.

"Marjorie. Marjorie A. Col—. I can't see the rest. Her name is—her name *was* Marjorie. And she bought something in Tampa," Noah lets out a huff and sits back in his chair. "That's it, guys. That's all I saw. Marjorie from Tampa."

Dane hops up from his seat and hovers over the table, looking at the picture Raven drew. He pushes his long hair behind his ears as he bends closer. Wrinkling his nose, he sniffs.

"I think...," he says. "I wonder if..."

"What? What?" Noah asks.

"I've had two episodes involving scents that seem to be perfumes or something. I'm wondering if they're related," he says.

Graham edges closer to his friend. "What other episode, Dane?" he asks.

"Well, the day before I came to Lee's house, I had a dream where two kids died at a nightclub. And the smell was sickly sweet mixed with something pungent. I didn't mention it to you guys in all the excitement of showing off my girl. Maybe Jack can check on it. We can let him know now that the woman—Marjorie—was from Tampa. And in the meantime, I'll track that scent. Noah? Be my light?"

Lee nods and makes his way back to the telephone, while Noah settles against the chair. Dane takes a seat next to his brother at the table. In seconds, they are both breathing deeply. On the couch, Raven closes her eyes, focusing on the sound of the Lightfoot boys as they track.

Graham watches Dane's head move slowly from side to side, up and down, and all around as he tracks, trying to trace the odors and smells that are constantly moving through the air. Like a bloodhound following a trail, Dane seems drawn by the scents. Finally, he sits still.

"Home," he whispers. But before he opens his eyes, he shouts, "Whoa!"

Graham nearly falls out of his chair. "What the—?" he says.

Noah's eyes fly open. They are not on his brother; they are on Raven. "Did you do that?" he asks her.

Raven looks aghast at the men, eyes wide. She bites her bottom lip and nods timidly.

Dane hops out of his chair and whirls around to face her. She cowers against the couch cushions. He rushes to her, leans down, and plants a sloppy kiss on her lips.

"That...was...*intense!*" he says.

Lee runs in from the other room to assess the commotion. Dane is laughing and whooping; Noah is staring at Raven with his chin on his chest; Graham is shaking his head in confusion.

"What has happened?" Lee says.

Dane turns around, and with a smile from ear to ear exclaims, "Hona, you'll never believe it. My future bride just sent a nuclear bomb of a beacon!" He pulls Raven to her feet for a bear hug that takes her breath away.

Lee regards Raven, then Noah.

"That she did," Noah says. "Brightest light I have ever seen. Congratulations Bird. You have officially passed your first beaconing session!"

"Well, before you all get too giddy on me, I need to let you know what Jack found out," Lee says. "There were two kids who died the other night at a local nightclub, just like you said, Dane. The police said they were both high on a drug called 'ecstasy' that compromised their systems."

"Does ecstasy have an odor?" Dane asks.

"Jack said it does not," Lee says.

"Then what did I smell?" Dane asks.

"Most likely, it was the combination of perfumes, lotions, and body odors from all the sweaty people dancing," Noah says.

"How did the kids die?" Raven asks.

"Now that is the perplexing part," Lee says. "According to Jack, they died of dehydration and heat exhaustion. Apparently, the drug inhibited their ability to sweat and cool themselves. When the medical examiner took their temperatures, they were so warm that they were feverish."

"What a horrible way to die," Raven says.

"Take ecstasy and die in agony," Noah says.

"What about Marjorie from Tampa?" Graham asks.

"Jack said he would check on that when he gets a chance, but since it is out of his jurisdiction, it is not going to be one of our cases; nevertheless, he will let the Tampa PD know that we are aware of the occurrence," Lee says.

Just then, Lee's pager sounds. He reads the display, and then he tucks it back on his belt. Sensing that he has stifled the mood, Lee shifts courses. "Well, I understand that there is a party happening tonight."

"A party? When?" Raven asks.

Before she can get an answer, there is a knock at the door. Dane hurries to answer it. He swings the door wide, and in sweeps Wren Thistleseed, followed by the rest of the girls—Shine, Selah, Zorah, Debby, and Shelly. "Surprise!" they shout in unison.

Shelly runs to Raven and puts her arms around her waist. Behind her, the others file in, loaded down with balloons, food, and packages.

"It's for you, Raven. We're having a cagement party for you," Shelly says. "But without a cage, I think."

Raven laughs and hugs the little girl. "Thanks, Sweetie. Where are the boys?"

"Oh, they had to stay home 'cause a cagement party is just for girls," Shelly says.

"That's right," Wren says, "so you men need to take your chicken and go home."

"Hey, this *is* my home," Dane says.

"I guess we will have to join the other males at the

Thistleseed home," Lee says, nonchalantly gathering the drawings from the table.

"Well, before we go, can I give the bride-to-be a gift, too?" Dane asks.

Reaching into his pocket, Dane pulls out a small cylindrical object covered in gold filigree and hands it to Raven. She turns it over in her hands, inspecting it with childlike wonder.

"Lipstick?" she asks.

"Not even close. Besides, you don't wear lipstick, Babe. Open it up."

She takes the cap off to reveal a sprayer. Lifting it to her nose, she smiles broadly. "*DeVanille!*" she exclaims. "My favorite fragrance." She spritzes a little on her wrists and rubs them together. Immediately, the scent of vanilla fills the room.

Graham sniffs the air. "So that's why you always smell like sugar cookies!"

"And since you don't ever carry a purse, you can slip this into your pocket or even carry it in one of your mocs," Dane says.

She throws her arms around his neck and gives him a resounding kiss, much to the delight of the guests. He is slow to pull away, keeping his eyes locked on Raven until Wren pulls on his shirt sleeve.

"And because we're throwing you out of your house, Dane, we got you a present," Wren says. She thrusts a wrapped box into his hands.

"Oh, I get it. We love you, Dane. Here's a gift. Now, get out," he says.

"Something like that," Shine teases. "Open it."

Dane tears the colorful paper off the package. Inside is a handsome square bottle of cologne. He pulls his mouth down in a quizzical expression.

"We know you don't wear cologne, but this one is special. Smell it," Selah says.

He twists open the cap and puts the bottle hesitantly to his nose. Taking a tentative sniff, his eyes widen, his mouth splits into a grin, and he cuts his eyes to Raven.

"Pretty neat," he says.

"It's called *Homme DeVanille.* It means 'Man of Vanilla.' They have similar ingredients, so they smell close to the same," Shine says.

"I can smell that, but this one is more masculine, right?" Dane says.

"Uh huh. We figured you could wear your 'smell pretty', and when you're away from Raven, you'll still be smelling her," Shelly says.

The room erupts in laughter at her choice of words, and Shelly looks crestfallen, but Dane bends down and kisses her on the cheek. "That is the most wonderful idea I have ever heard, Shell. You are a genius. I'm gonna put some on right now!" He dabs a little on his finger and wipes it on his neck.

Shelly's little face lights up at the compliment, and she skips away to her mother's side. Lee pushes the men—who seem decidedly loathe to go—out the door, leaving the girls to their party. As he pulls the door closed, Dane blows a kiss to Raven, wishing he could shoo everyone away and have her all to himself. *Plenty of time for that later,* he thinks rationally, but his irrational mind nags, *I want her now.*

Watching him leave, Raven feels her face flush. She fans herself with her hand, breathing in the scent of the heavenly fragrance on her tingling wrists.

CHAPTER FIVE
TO TAMPA

THE DAYS SEEM TO BE MOVING so quickly, Raven marvels. She adjusts her seat and leans back just a little. It feels good to relax and take a break from the exhausting training of the past week. She is just beginning to realize what a toll it takes on her—both physically and mentally. She stretches her long legs out before her, pushing the seat back as far as it will go.

"Get comfy, Babe," Dane says. "It's a pretty long ride to Tampa. Let me know when you need a rest stop. There's plenty on the way."

"I'm fine, honey. It's not like I've never taken a long car trip before. I moved here from Arizona, you know," Raven says.

"I know. But, you know, not with me or anything, and I just want you to be comfortable and all, and…" Dane blathers.

"Dane. I'm fine! I have Diet Coke, pretzels, a pillow, a blanket, and a neat book from my mother about Hopi Katsinas to look at. What more do I need?"

"A good driver?" He grins at her.

"You bet. I have the best driver in the world." She leans over to give him a nuzzling kiss on the cheek, and he inhales her sweet aroma.

"You smell good," he says. "Want to take a short smooch break before we leave?"

She laughs aloud. "I don't know what's with you lately, but you're like a desert nomad who can't get enough water!"

"I'm sorry, but you look and smell so enticing, it takes all my self-control not to attack you every time you're near." He presents his best chastised child look from beneath his lashes.

"Well, keep it in check, Bucko. We've got plenty of time for that. Let's get on the road."

"Your wish is my command." He gives an exaggerated sigh and pulls out onto the street.

Raven snaps her seatbelt in place and reclines against the headrest, her left arm slung lazily across the back of Dane's neck. She wonders about his increase in ardor ever since the engagement party. But then, she has had the same desires. Never before having a steady boyfriend, her love for Dane is unlike any feeling she has ever experienced. She lifts her right hand to push against her bangs, and as she does, her wrist passes close to her nose. She inhales. *I love this scent, and I love this man.* She raises her left knee and reaches into the side of her moccasin, retrieving the lipstick shaped perfume container. She dislodges the cap with her nimble fingers, brings it to the hollow of her neck, and presses the top slightly. Instantly, the essence of vanilla fills the car.

"Babe, I'm gonna have to get you another one of those perfumes before the week is out," Dane says. "I bet you've almost used it up."

"I'm sorry. It smells so good, I can't seem to get enough of it," she says.

"As long as it makes you happy," he says, reaching over to fondle her knee.

She smiles and replaces the top on the canister. *I better go easy on this. Don't know how much it cost him.*

"New mocs?" he asks, changing the conversation.

She raises her feet to display her most recent footwear. "My mother sent them, along with this book. They're made of yucca plants instead of leather. She thinks they'll be more comfortable in South Florida," she says, admiring the twisted honey-colored fibers laced with soft leather strips. Looking at the shoes makes Raven think about her mother, Robin, one of Prescott, Arizona's finest artisans. She crafts both leather and yucca fiber moccasins and makes decorated pine needle and bark strip baskets so tightly-woven that they hold water. Raven is fiercely proud of her mother's talents. Out of respect and to honor her, Raven only wears the many handmade pairs of moccasins her mother sends every few months.

"I can't wait to meet her," Dane says.

"Soon," Raven says. "And then you'll have a closet full of moccasins, too."

The trip passes relatively quickly, with small talk and an occasional pit stop, and before they know it, they are seeing signs for Tampa on I-4. Raven notices patches of uprooted oaks and broken palm trees along the roadside, as well as some mangled billboards, and she points them out.

"Spinoff from Hurricane Andrew this past August," he says. "See that twisted light post? That's from tornado activity. And those trees leaning over—horizontal wind shear. Funny, isn't it? The pine trees don't snap like the hardwoods. They bend. They'll stay bent, too."

"Why didn't your mother evacuate? Isn't it dangerous to be so near a hurricane?"

"She won't leave that village. It's been her home for the past ten years. She doesn't have much family other than us boys. A distant aunt that's a storyteller or something, and maybe an uncle or cousin who wrestles alligators."

"She never remarried after your father died?"

"Nope. Never did. Said nobody interested her, but I sometimes wonder if there was another guy, and she just didn't want us kids to be upset. She won't say. Stubborn, you know."

"Yes, I seem to know someone else like that."

Dane feigns shock and slaps his cheek. "*Moi?* You surely don't mean me, do you?"

"Duh! Oh, look. There's our exit for the Tampa PD." Dane maneuvers the car off the interstate highway, following the signs to lead them to the Tampa Police Department. Lee has already called ahead and spoken with the Chief of Police about the recent death of Marjorie from Tampa. Dane and Raven hope to gather information that may tie her death to that of the two kids in Tallahassee, and to their recent unsettling tracks.

Inside the Chief's office, Raven and Dane sit on round-backed molded plastic chairs, meant to look modern, but feeling much less so. The walls are covered with plaques and framed certificates of commendation, photographs, and dozens of yellow stick-on notes.

Chief Lew Rowan is a large, rotund man with salt-and-pepper hair and narrow squared-off sideburns. His face is tanned and wrinkled, and startling green eyes shine from above high, round cheeks. His frame fills the massive leather office chair which creaks as he rocks it slowly back and forth. At first sight an imposing character, one's intimidation at his appearance fades when he speaks. His voice is soft and pleasant, and his smile is contagious. Raven likes him immediately, and he seems equally charmed by her.

"I got the call from Mr. Thistleseed, and I did some checking," Chief Rowan says, spreading papers from an opened file on his desk. "The lady in question was named Marjorie Alice Collier. And she was quite the Tampa Bay socialite. Came from a wealthy family. You're familiar with Collier County? That's her kin folk. Anyhow, Miss Marjorie was found five days ago in her home by her housekeeper. She had been dead for several hours—since the night before, apparently. They found her lying on a mess of broken bottles. It appeared that she exsanguinated—bled out. Let's see, here."

He rifles through some papers and selects a report. Raven shifts in her uncomfortable seat. The room is hot, and her bangs are beginning to stick to her forehead.

Chief Rowan smiles up at her from the desk. "Here we go. M.E.'s report. Some Medical Examiner mumbo jumbo...Blah, blah, blah...posterior trauma...length of cuts...O.K. here it is. Stomach contents. Says she had consumed approximately five liters of wine. Now why don't they say ounces or cups? I hate this metric stuff. How much is five liters?"

"Five of those big bottles, I'd say," Raven offers.

"I'd say that, too, little lady. Now wouldn't that have been easier? To say she drank five bottles of wine? And that would be, like 30 glasses or so. That beats my record! Well, anyway. Let's see. Toxicology. Here's the thing—as if five bottles of wine wouldn't kick your butt—she's dosed up on ecstasy."

"Ecstasy?" Dane says. "Our victims in Tallahassee

had taken ecstasy, too."

"Searched her place but couldn't find any evidence. No wrappers, no pills. But it was all in her system. Poor Marjorie. Lookin' for a party but died all by herself." Chief Rowan shakes his head and shrugs.

"Take ecstasy and die in agony," Raven says.

"What's that?" the Chief asks.

"Something my brother said, but it's pretty true. I'd say she died a very painful death," Dane says.

The Chief nods his massive head somberly. "Bad way to die, too."

"But what really killed her? Was it the drug or the alcohol?" Raven asks.

"That's a very good question, young lady. I'd say both, and I'd be right—and wrong. What do you know about ecstasy?"

"Not much, really. It makes you—uh—you get—I really don't know," Raven admits.

Chief Rowan laughs at her attempt to explain. "It makes you horny. Is that what you meant to say?"

"Yes, I guess," she says, brushing invisible lint from her khaki shorts.

"It does do that, as well as a long list of other things. People say it makes colors vivid, sounds clear, smells, tastes, etc. more psychedelic. Just enhances all your senses. And it makes you feel like you are sexy and alluring. Messes with your inhibitions. Now that, in itself, is not so bad. It's the side effects that get you. Vomiting, paranoia, panic attacks, hallucinations, severe dehydration. Not my idea of a good time."

"So, did the ecstasy kill her?" Dane asks.

"Not according to this report. It says she died from hyponatraemia."

"And that is…" Dane prompts.

"Liquid poisoning," Chief Rowan replies.

"Liquid poison? You mean like drain cleaner or something?" Raven asks.

"No. Liquid poison-ING. From drinking too much liquid," he says.

"How is that possible? I've never heard of drinking too much liquid, unless it's too much alcohol. Was it alcohol poisoning?" Raven asks.

"You'd think so. I wondered the same thing, so I asked my M.E. He said that drinking excessive water or fluid disturbs the sodium balance in the body and makes the organs swell. And the brain, since it can't expand inside the skull, gets all compressed. That puts pressure on the brain stem and—boom—coma leading to death. That's what killed Miss Marjorie. Those five *metric liters* of wine she drank because the ecstasy made her hot and thirsty," Chief Rowan says.

Raven's mouth is dry from all the talk about dehydration and drinking. *What I wouldn't give for a Diet Coke right now*, she thinks. She reaches into her pants pocket and takes out another pack of gum—the third pack of *Juicy Fruit* she's opened today. She puts two sticks into her mouth and chews vigorously, nervously. Seeing the Chief watching her, she extends the pack of gum to him.

"Don't mind if I do," he says, extracting one silver-papered stick.

For a few moments they sit looking at each other, chewing like two cows in a field. Dane breaks the silence by getting to his feet and reaching out to the Chief.

"Thank you, sir, for your help," he says, grasping the big man's hand.

"Not at all. I'll fax a copy to your department in Tallahassee later today," Chief Rowan replies. He gives Raven a radiant smile. "And thank you for brightening my day."

Raven lets him engulf her slender hand with both of his. "You're very welcome."

"You kids stay clear of the trees while you're here. We've still got limbs falling all over the place," Chief Rowan says as he begins gathering up the mess of papers spread on the desk.

Back at the car, Raven's first order of business is to open the small cooler and take out a can of cold soda for herself and one for Dane. "All that talk in there made me so thirsty, I thought I was going to dry up in the chair." She chugs nearly half the can, then lets out a healthy burp, much to her own surprise.

"Such a lady," Dane snorts, laughing.

"Oh, just shut up and drive," she retorts, anxious to get to the village and meet her future mother-in-law.

Fortunately, the drive is short, and within a few minutes, they see the water tower with a huge arrow through the tank that signals their turn off from I-4. As they arrive in front of the Seminole Village and Culture Center, Raven squirms in her seat.

"Do I look O.K.?" she asks.

"You look perfect," Dane says leaning in for a kiss.

He gets out and rounds the car to open her door. Raven reaches into her moccasin and retrieves the *DeVanille* canister, giving herself another quick spray. Satisfied that she looks and smells presentable, she exits the car and approaches the door on the arm of her handsome sweetheart.

CHAPTER SIX
FAWN LIGHTFOOT

ENTERING THE SEMINOLE INDIAN GIFT SHOP on the way to the Museum is like stepping back in time. Raven marvels at the pictures and the décor, but, most of all, she notices the colors. Patchwork skirts, jackets, and extra-long shirts hang along the walls, their patterns seeming to move like rivers or snakes or running animals. Red, yellow, white, and black dominate the color palate. She is fascinated, and her eyes feel dry from holding them open so wide. Light through the windows catches on racks of earrings and necklaces made of tiny glass seed beads, sending showers of multicolored fireflies dancing about the room. The smell of smoldering sage tickles her nose.

Dane leads her through the room, while smiling and nodding to the woman sitting beside the counter. She is white-haired, dark-skinned, and wrinkled, with row upon row of seed bead necklaces encircling her neck from shoulders to chin. A short translucent cape covers her bodice and bare arms, ending with a ruffle just below her waist. Her skirt is full, with patchwork patterns on different colored backgrounds of horizontal stripes.

Some of the patterns are triangular, some are blocks, and yet others look like the capital letter "T" alternately upright and upside down. The effect is mesmerizing. The old woman's wrinkles bunch together beside her mouth to reveal a broad smile. She waves as they pass through the back door.

Stepping out the door and into the sunlight, Raven's breath catches at the sight of her surroundings. Directly in front of them, in the center of the area, stands the *Coo-Taun Cho-Bee* Museum. It is a massive structure, shaped like an eight-sided star. Around the perimeter runs a wooded pathway, and on the outskirts of the pathway are the most unusual buildings Raven has ever seen. They are open pavilions, like Tiki-huts, but different. The roofs are thatched with palm leaves. Some of the buildings are rounded; some are square. But all are exposed to the elements, with raised platforms in the center and open shelves between the outer posts.

Within the buildings are people—women dressed as the old woman in the shop, men in slacks and long colorful knee-length shirts, and quite a few children—some dressed as the adults, and others shirtless and barefoot, playing with each other or with long-tailed, smooth-haired dogs. Raven laughs aloud.

"What's so funny?" Dane asks.

"Nothing is funny. It's just wonderful!" she says, clapping her hands together.

He hugs her to him. *How like a child she is sometimes.* He wishes he could see things through her eyes. The village is just another village to him, but to her, it's a magical world. Just then, he hears a commotion from beyond the Museum.

"Mom!" he calls.

Fawn Lightfoot appears on the boardwalk. She is tall, perhaps even taller than Raven, and stately, with perfect posture and a relaxed composure. Her face is alight with the afternoon sun as she looks toward them. She walks with her arms outstretched, and Dane runs to embrace her. Raven hangs back, a little unsure of herself, but then Fawn strides forward to throw her arms around her future daughter-in-law. The hug is strong and fierce, as if the women have known each other forever.

"Daughter," Fawn says. "I'm happy you are here, at last."

Raven pulls back and gazes into the older woman's face. Fawn's onyx-colored eyes are so familiar. *Of course—Noah.* There is no mistaking their resemblance, but she also sees Dane in that beautiful face. Fawn's eyebrows pull down in a tiny frown, and then her eyes open wide.

"You smell like cookies!" she says with a huge smile.

The three of them laugh at the statement, and there are no strangers among them anymore. Fawn pulls Dane to one side and Raven to the other, takes their hands, and walks them to her *chickee*—one of the thatched roof houses that surround the Museum. They sit on the platform, and she pours them tall glasses of fresh, cold water with crushed mint leaves. A loud honking noise draws Raven's attention. She looks over Fawn's shoulder and sees a large, grey goose waddling toward the platform. Fawn reaches down and strokes the goose's long neck.

"This is Emma. She thinks I'm her mother, and I guess I am. She follows me everywhere. It's a mutually beneficial relationship. I give her treats, and she keeps the bugs away from my *chickee*," she says, throwing a handful of ground corn on the ground for the goose.

"Chickee, like little chickens?" Raven asks.

Fawn laughs brightly. "No, sweetie. A *chickee* is an open- sided house, but sometimes little chickens—and a big goose—run through it."

"Is this your home?" Raven asks.

"This is more of a demonstration village, meant to show visitors how the Seminoles live. I do my sewing and basketry here. My *chickee*—the one I live in—is much bigger but built the same. There are about 40 of us who live in the village, just behind that fence. I have curtains in mine for privacy, but some of the other families don't use curtains. We just don't look."

"Mom says she doesn't look, but I don't believe her."

"Boy, you hold your tongue. You're not too old to whip," Fawn laughs, reaching up to pat her hair.

"Is that your hair, or is that a hat?" Raven asks.

"Speaks her mind, this one, doesn't she?" Fawn says. "That's a good quality, Raven. Always say what you want to say. I admire that in a man and a woman."

Raven smiles, feeling at ease with the woman, but still examining the unusual hairdo.

"O.K., I'll give you the short version. Seminole women used to wear their hair long and loose in the beginning, but it was impractical when they moved down south, so they began twisting their hair into buns on the top of their heads. Somewhere along the way, after seeing white women wearing hats and bonnets to shade their faces, someone got the idea to make a hairdo that worked like a hat. It takes two people to fix it. One person leans over while the other one combs the hair forward to the crown of the head and secures it like a ponytail. Then a form is placed either just behind or in front of the ponytail. At first the women used a rolled-up piece of hide, but now we make our own forms in different shapes out of soft wire, fabric, or starched cloth. Once the form is placed, it is pinned to the scalp with bobbypins. Then the ponytail is fanned out and woven into the shape, just like you weave a basket. The ends of the hair are pushed under the form and pinned to keep it tight. Ta-da. You now have a hair hat!"

"Can I..." Raven begins.

"...touch it? Of course. In fact, it's almost closing time, so I'm going to take it down. You can help me," Fawn says.

Dane watches the two women bonding—sharing stories, getting to know each other, becoming mother and daughter without even trying, and his heart swells. As Raven gently unweaves Fawn's hair from the form, he thinks back to a time when his mother was not so happy—to the time when his father was killed.

* * *

Fawn had taken him to the Berry *Pvsktv*—fasting celebration—in North Florida. Dane played with the other children and their dogs and had a great time. There were lots of grownups milling around, but he paid little heed to them. Playing behind the old men's arbor, Dane heard the elders talking about his gift, and he wondered what gift that might be. It was not close to his birthday, and Mom hadn't mentioned anything about a party, so he dismissed it to old people not knowing anything. After all, he was ten years old, and they were ancient.

The ride home the next day was long, but Dane lay on the seat with his bare feet in his mother's lap and listened to her telling stories. She told about the crows that had colorful feathers and sang so wonderfully that everyone else in the forest would be quiet just to listen to them. One day, the crows saw something bright orange on the ground below and a black cloud up above it in the sky. They flew to a blackened tree to investigate, climbing higher and higher until the limb broke. The crows fell to the ground and were burned. Their feathers were turned black by the soot and charcoal, and the smoke hurt their throats so much they could only say, "Caw. Caw."

"That was a fire, Mama," Dane said.

"That's right. Fire is powerful. We respect it, and we never play with it," Fawn said.

She told him the story of the Little People who lived among the trees and came to the bedside of sick people to help them get better. The Little People were afraid of storms and hid in the trees when the thunder sounded. The thunder and lightning chased them all around the trees, but the Little People escaped by disappearing into holes in the trees.

"And that's why you never stand under a tree in a storm," Dane said.

"Or you might get hit by lightning," Fawn said.

His favorite was the story of Possum and his lovely tail. It was so fluffy and full, and he would say to the other animals that his tail was so much better than theirs. One day, the other animals decided to trick him. They told him that his tail could be even more beautiful if he would wrap tree moss around it for a few days. Possum was so vain that he did exactly that. But when he unwrapped the moss, he was so sad. All the hair had fallen off, and it never grew back.

"That's why you don't brag and boast," Dane said.

And through the old stories, young Dane Lightfoot learned right from wrong.

After the long ride, Dane was glad to get back to his home. It was cold up there at Pine Arbor, and Dane was used to the balmy South Florida weather and his breezy *chickee* home. To tell the truth, he missed his brothers and sisters, even though they were all much older than he. His father was old, too, but Dane loved to follow him around watching him make medicine and heal sick people. *I will be a heles-pocase medicine man, too, one day*, he decided.

The next afternoon after he returned, Dane was sitting on the ground whittling a stick when he sensed someone inside the *chickee*. Looking around the pole, he glimpsed a man moving the bedding blankets. The man had his back to him, but Dane could see the four-foot rattlesnake he held behind its triangular-shaped head. The man stuffed the snake head-first into the blankets, and then hurriedly left the hut. Dane knew the danger the snake presented, so he ran to find his mother.

When the two of them ran back to the hut, they saw his father lying on the ground. The snake was still coiled after striking Joe Lightfoot in the neck. Fawn screamed and beat the snake with the mallet she used to grind corn. Dane couldn't move. Eyes wide, he watched his father squirm and twist on the ground. Suddenly, a man came running in with a bag of healing herbs. What? Another *heles-pocase?* Dane recognized him as the medicine man from Pine Arbor. *What was he doing there?* As if he heard him, the man whipped his head around and stared at Dane. Suddenly, his father shook all over and convulsed, then he lay still—dead.

"Father!" Dane shouted, his cries mingling with the screams of his mother.

The other medicine man put his arms around Dane's mother, but Dane ran forward and pushed him away. He remembered the man's eyes. They were blue—so blue, they were almost white. Silver eyes. Evil eyes.

His mother didn't smile for a long, long time. Until Noah was born.

* * *

"Dane, I asked you how Noah is," Fawn says.

Dane looks at his mother. Her hair hangs in a long braid down her back, and he realizes he has been daydreaming. "Sorry. He's good, Mom. Loving his Chief Osceola role at the football games. It suits him, you know. He lives for the roar of the crowd."

"That boy has always been one for attention," Fawn agrees. "Listen, you two. I have to get my supplies put away and tidied up for tomorrow. Why don't you take a tour around the grounds while there's some daylight left? I'll catch up with you in a few minutes."

Dane pulls Raven to her feet. "Good idea, Mom. This one needs some exercise."

"Ha," Raven says, but she is glad to move around. Her muscles are sore from riding, and her arms and legs are stiff. She clasps Dane's hand and listens as he gives her the walking tour.

They stroll on the wooden pathway past the arts and crafts *chickees* and make their way to a large sand-filled pit. Raven leans near the edge to get a better look below.

"Not too close, Babe. That's an alligator pit," Dane says. She pulls back abruptly, and he laughs heartily.

"Don't worry, Honey. It's for alligator wrestling demonstrations. The real gators are in lairs farther back. The People call them *'Hal Pa Te.'* There's one old snapper back there called 'Big Joe.' He's over ten feet long."

Raven punches him in the arm. "Don't do that again."

"Yes ma'am. Do keep your eyes open, though, because there are animals living in the wild around the village. If you look carefully, you may see bobcats, a Florida panther, deer, giant tortoises, and maybe even a black bear."

"I grew up in the mountains of Arizona. There were few trees, a little bit of grass, and lots of rocks. It almost feels claustrophobic here. The landscape surrounds you, and it's so close. And hot. Ye gads, it's hot. How come you aren't sweating like me?"

"I guess I'm used to the heat. We'll get you a drink of water in the Museum."

They enter the *Coo-Taun Cho-Bee* Museum, and Raven instantly relaxes. *Ah, air conditioning!* Locating a water fountain near the door, she drinks deeply at first, but then she remembers what Chief Lew Rowan said about drinking too much. She stops in mid- gulp, and then slowly takes a few more mouthfuls. *Better.*

Fawn is already inside the Museum waiting on them. She puts her arm around Raven's waist and walks her through the Seminole history exhibits.

"Back in 1979, there was a construction crew building a parking garage in this location. While they were excavating, they began to uncover the skeletons of lots of people. When the authorities investigated, they determined the bones to be the remains of 150 Indians who fought and died during the Seminole Wars in the 1800s. The Seminole Nation declared the site a sacred ancestral burial ground and had the construction halted.

After much debate and bargaining, the Seminoles settled for this seven and one-half acre tract of land in which to rebury and consecrate our ancestors' remains. They are buried beneath this very Museum. This became known as Seminole Indian Village. In 1989, we built the Bingo Palace and Smoke Shop. Seminole Medicine Man Bobby Henry runs the village and does alligator wrestling shows sometimes. He's also a rainmaker," Fawn explains.

"He can make it rain?" Raven asks.

"So, they say," Dane says. "I've never seen it, but Mom swears that he can."

"Wow! This is so interesting," Raven says, yawning.

"Yes, it is. But you are tired, and so am I. Let's go to

my home, and I will fix you an authentic Seminole supper," Fawn says, leading Raven out the door. "Come, Emma," she tells the goose, who falls in step behind them.

The walk to Fawn's house is short—just beyond the wooden fence that surrounds the demonstration area. It is exactly as she described it—a larger version of her demo *chickee*. Raven finds it charming and surprisingly cool with the breeze blowing through the open walls. The outer curtains hang about a foot from the ceiling crossbeams and fall all the way to the packed dirt floor. They mimic the patterns in the colorful clothing hanging in the gift shop. The open tops allow the breeze to flow into the partitioned "rooms" and throughout the interior.

Inside the *chickee*, lightweight curtains meet in the center of the structure to form a cross, dividing the area into four quadrants. One section is outfitted with typical kitchen appliances, as well as a large, deep, cast-iron pot on a propane-fed burner. Of the other three sections, one is clearly a bathroom—made private with plywood along the outside. The others are multi-purpose rooms, with raised platforms that can be used as beds or seating areas. Many woven baskets are stacked beneath the platforms and throughout the residence and are filled with bedding, clothing, and other household necessities.

"Son, since I know you two aren't sleeping together, you take the room on the left, and Raven can sleep in my room with me. Why don't you go ahead and get your overnight things, and Raven can help me start cooking," Fawn says, giving Raven a wink.

"Uh, yeah, sure thing, Mom." He grins, knowing Raven's lack of culinary skills. Walking backwards, he waves and blows his fiancé a kiss.

"A wink and a kiss. Aren't I the lucky one?" Raven laughs and rolls her eyes.

Fawn pulls a stool up and directs Raven to sit and watch while she begins the cooking.

"Tonight, we will have Seminole tacos," she says. When Raven makes a confused face, she explains. "Not really tacos. I'm going to teach you to make fry bread. First, we fire up the propane burner. This is vegetable oil. We've got to get it really hot. While it's heating, we mix and pat out the bread."

Into a large bowl Fawn adds flour, salt, and water, mixing the dough with her hand until it pulls away from the sides of the bowl. She uses no measuring cups. This is a technique learned from years of practice. She adds more flour to keep the dough from being too sticky. When it gets to the consistency she likes, she pulls off a handful and begins slapping it back and forth between her floured hands until it is a large, flat pancake the size of a dinner plate and about an inch thick.

Carefully, she slides the bread into the hot oil, and then begins forming another one. She slides another one in the oil and flips the first one over with tongs. When she adds the next one, she removes the first one—now floating on the surface. There is a silent rhythm to her cooking, and Raven is mesmerized, almost hypnotized by her fluid motions. It seems like mere moments have passed, but Fawn has removed all the breads from the oil and transferred them to a brown paper bag to drain the grease and keep them warm.

Dane returns and hands Raven a Diet Coke, then sits on the floor beside her watching his mother cook. This has always been one of his favorite activities. He is totally at peace tonight.

Fawn opens the refrigerator and pulls out a container of precut vegetables—carrots, wild onions, yellow squash, and green pole beans. After adding lard to a cast iron skillet, she dumps all the raw vegetables in and lets them sizzle. In another skillet, she browns up ground venison. The aroma of the food is rich, and Raven's stomach growls. She realizes now how hungry she is.

"Dane. Plates, please," Fawn says.

He jumps up and removes plates, coffee cups, and spoons from a shelf over the oven. He lays them out on the "guest bed," as this is also the table when company visits. Fawn brings the paper sack and a big splatter ware pot over to the platform. She has combined all the vegetables and the meat in the pot and has also added some red beans. In an enamel coffee kettle on another burner, a yellow mixture bubbles. She brings the kettle over and fills their cups with it. Onto each plate, she places a huge piece of fry bread, and then covers it with the meat and vegetable mixture.

"May I bless it?" Dane asks.

Fawn raises her eyebrows, but she says nothing, simply nods her head.

"Father, for what we are about to receive, make us truly thankful, and bless us on our journeys and in our daily lives. In Jesus' name. Amen."

"Now?" Fawn asks.

"Dive in," Dane says.

Raven, unsure of how to proceed, watches the others. Seeing Dane fold up the fry bread and topping like a taco, she follows suit. The result is a mouthful of soft, yet crispy bread, succulent meat, and crunchy vegetables. Nearly half of the topping plops onto the plate, and Raven quickly looks up, embarrassed. She is relieved to note that the others have substantial amounts of topping on their plates, too. They take their spoons and scoop it back onto their bread before each bite.

"Delicious," Raven says through a mouthful.

"Try the *sofkee*," Dane says pointing to the mug of steaming yellow mush.

"What is it?" Raven asks.

"Try it first, then I'll tell you."

"It's not cats or dogs or something weird, is it?"

Fawn drops her fry bread and laughs cheerfully. "It's just ground corn mixed with water, Raven. Try it. If you don't like it, you don't have to finish it."

Raven picks up the mug and sniffs the drink, then takes a tentative sip. The flavor is deceiving. What looks like thick yellow sludge is actually sweet and hearty.

"This is really good!" she says, taking a bigger gulp. Before she knows it, she has emptied the cup. "May I...?"

Fawn jumps to grab the kettle and refills Raven's mug, delighted that she likes the traditional Seminole drink. The three of them spend the remainder of the time eating, drinking, and becoming a family. After all of the meat and vegetables are finished, the dishes are washed and dried, and the leftover fry bread is rolled up in the bag, they are full and completely talked out.

Fawn scoops out the remainder of the *sofkee* and tosses it outside for her large grey goose, who honks loudly and gratefully. "Emma will sleep out there and alert us to any animal or human intruders," she assures them.

Raven changes into boxer shorts and a t-shirt and washes her hands and face in the bathroom. She thinks briefly about reapplying her perfume but rejects the idea. It's with her moccasins in a basket in the sleeping area, and she's tired. When she comes out, she sees that Fawn has changed into a cotton nightdress and has covered the platform with several thick blankets, topped by a lightweight quilt. Fawn gives her a quick hug and kiss, and then she climbs up on one side of the platform "bed."

Take your time getting into bed, Raven. We don't follow a clock," she says.

"I won't be long, Fawn. I'm really tired," Raven says.

"Me, too," Dane says behind her.

Raven turns and folds herself into his arms for a kiss. He holds her tightly for a long time before pushing her away. "I love you, Babe," he says.

"I love you, too, Dane."

Turning her around, he pushes her toward her room, and then he draws the curtains around the outside of the *chickee* before entering his own room.

"Mom?" Dane says.

"A story?" Fawn responds.

"Creation," he says, settling himself on the blankets of his platform bed.

Fawn's voice is soft but clear through the hanging curtains as she begins the story. It has always been Dane's favorite. She tells it to him every time he visits, and he never grows tired of it.

"In the beginning of time, the Muskogee People were born out of Mother Earth. Her children crawled up through a hole in the ground like a colony of ants. The People all lived together beside the tall mountains that reached up to the sky in the lands of the west. But there were so many of The People, it was difficult for friends and even families to have alliances with each other.

One day, *Hesaketvmese*—Master of Breath—sent a thick fog upon the earth, and The People could not see. They called out to each other in fear as they wandered around.

They were as the blind. They drifted apart and became lost. Whenever they came upon another person, they would cling to that person, and in this way The People soon began to form small groups for security.

Finally, Father Spirit took pity on them and began to blow the fog away. He blew His breath first from the eastern edge of the world, where the sun rises. He blew until the world was clear again, and The People could see. The People swore eternal brotherhood within their small groups and promised to be like large families—like brother and sister, mother and daughter, father and son. And then The People sang a hymn of thanksgiving to the Master of Breath for His wisdom.

Those that were the farthest to the lands of the east were the first group to see the sun. They praised the wind that blew the fog away and called themselves the Wind Clan. The next group called themselves the Bear Clan, for that was the first animal they saw when the fog disappeared.

Other groups also gave themselves names, choosing the name of the first thing they saw when the fog passed away from them. In this way, their groups came to be known as the clans of Snake and Panther, of Toad and Bird, of Deer and Alligator; Beaver and Otter, Tiger and Wolf, Raccoon, and Sweet Potato…"

"…but the Wind Clan remained the most important clan of all," Dane says, finishing the story. "Good night, Mom."

"Good night, my son."

Neither of them must bid Raven a good night, for she is already sound asleep. The Florida night is warm, the breeze off the bay is constant, and the family in Fawn Lightfoot's *chickee* is at peace—at last.

CHAPTER SEVEN
CEDAR WOMAN'S GIFTS

DANE AWAKENS TO PLEASANT SMELLS for a change—food and fresh air. He puts on his jeans and passes through the curtain into the kitchen where Fawn stands stirring a pot of stew. Emma pokes her long neck into the room. Fawn throws her a handful of corn, shooing her out of the house. Dane snickers at them. Seeing him, she smiles and reaches for the coffee pot.

"Coffee?" she asks.

"No thanks, Mom. Don't drink it anymore. How about some *sofkee*, if your goose doesn't mind? I don't get that at home."

"Emma knows her place. *Sofkee*, it is. I'll send some of the ground corn back with Raven with very detailed instructions on how to make it."

"Better show me how to make it. Raven's not much

of a cook." He grins broadly.

Fawn fills a steaming mug with the corn and water mixture, and then she pours herself a cup of coffee. They sit facing each other, blowing across the tops of their cups to cool the liquids inside. After a few moments, Fawn puts her mug down and covers Dane's hand with her own.

"Son, your girl is sick," Fawn says.

"What?"

Dane frowns at his mother, but he knows she must be right. She's always right about illnesses. Fawn does not have second sight, but she learned from her mother at a young age how to diagnose and treat people using local plants and herbs. It is both her calling and her special gift. Though she has no medical degree, the villagers come to her for advice and herbal cures. She is Cedar Woman—the village healer.

"What's wrong with her?" Dane asks.

"Something poisons her from the inside. She needs healing," she says.

"What makes you so positive, Mom? Are you sure she's not just overtired from the trip, and from the training?"

"Training? Does she have the gift?" Fawn asks, startled.

"She does. As Noah says, 'she's eat up with it'. But she doesn't know how to use it yet, so we've been training her. You know how taxing that is on your mind and your body."

"Oh, yes. It's been all around me—my dad, your dad, Jimbo, you, Noah, others I know."

"Well, then you understand. Maybe Raven is just overwhelmed."

"Dane, she slept so hot last night that I had to move away. I felt her fever, heard her rapid breathing, smelled the poison coming through her skin. Her eyes are too bright, and her pupils are dilated. She needs cleansing," Fawn insists.

"Mom, I can't just give her black drink or take her out back to the sweat hut. We have to go back to Tallahassee today. She'd puke all the way home."

"And get rid of the sickness..."

"No. I'll get her to a doctor when we get home." "I can call the *heles-pocase*..."

"Mom. I love you, but sometimes you push so hard. Please. Let me deal with it," he says, his tone softening.

"You are so stubborn," she says. "You'd think we were bull clan instead of wind!"

"And who did I get that from?" He laughs and pats her hand.

"Good morning," Raven says, pushing aside the curtain. "I thought I was in another country for a minute. What language were you speaking?"

Dane jumps up and embraces her, ushering her to a chair at the table.

"Good morning, sweetheart. We were speaking Muskogee. It's the language of the Creeks and some of the

Florida Seminole tribes. It's not used much anymore outside the reservation and villages like this one. Did you rest well?" Fawn says.

"I slept like the dead!" Raven says. "I can't remember sleeping that soundly in a long time. I guess I was really tired."

Fawn has already poured a mug of *sofkee* for Raven and begins boiling a pot of water into which she crumbles dried herbs from an assortment of small baskets above the cooking station. She quickly brings the cooking pots from the stove and sets them on the table, along with the warmed fry bread from the previous evening.

"This is breakfast," she says. "Not your typical bacon and eggs, but I think you'll like it."

As before, Raven watches the others to see how to eat the food. Dane loads his plate with a fragrant yellow-orange blend from the large pot.

"This is buttered squash and pumpkin. It's a little like apple butter or jam. Try some," he says. He takes a piece of fry bread and dips it into the pureed mixture, using his spoon to push it up onto the bread. "Do it like this—like sopping a biscuit in gravy."

Raven tries the technique and finds it relatively simple. The squash and pumpkin are heavenly—sweet and savory at the same time. She is surprised to realize she is still famished.

The next pot contains something that smells similar

to spinach or collard greens. Fawn dips it out with a large spoon into a bowl and sets it beside Raven's plate.

"We call this *taal-holelke*—boiled swamp cabbage. It comes from the bud of the sabal palmetto. In the grocery store, you would call it 'hearts of palm.' We harvest it right here in a garden next to the village," Fawn says.

Raven's eyes roll when she tastes the cabbage. "It's wonderful! I've had hearts of palm, but they were pickled. This is so much better."

Fawn turns back to the pot boiling on the burner. She strains the herbs which have been steeped into the water and pours the tea into another mug, to which she adds a fat chunk of honeycomb. She sets the mug before Raven.

"Try this, Raven. I think you will find it pleasing," she says. Dane scowls at his mother, but she is nonplussed. Stubborn should be her middle name. This is one of Fawn's special medicinal teas, and she is determined to heal Raven's illness.

Raven takes the mug between her hands and breathes in the fragrant herbal blend. The heat of the water is melting the honeycomb, infusing its sweetness into the tea. She drinks deeply, and then she breathes out and long, "Aaahhhhhh." After few more mouthfuls of food, she drains the mug and smiles. Her face is one of sublime contentment. Color washes across her nose and cheeks. She wipes the moisture from beneath her nose.

Fawn is satisfied with the result. Her healing tea is

working, sweating the poison from Raven's body, bringing her internal systems back into harmony.

"I think I will send this recipe home with you. A cup every morning will start your day out right," she says.

"Thank you! Um—how about the *sofkee*, too?" Raven says.

"Done," Fawn laughs.

"Mom, I hate to say it, but we've got to get on the road. This was a quick pleasure-mixed-with-business trip, but we wanted to see you," Dane says.

Fawn looks down at the floor for a moment, then lifts her face to the young couple in a radiant smile, nodding. They all exchange hugs, and then Raven leaves the room to get changed.

As soon as Raven is out of earshot, Fawn turns to Dane. "You will give her this tea each morning, Dane. It will cleanse her system. Don't defy me, Son. It may save her life."

A chill tickles the back of Dane's neck. His mother is rarely wrong in matters of life and death. He nods, and then pulls his mother close, holding his lips against her cheek before going into the bedroom.

Fawn busies herself with gathering the ingredients for the *sofkee* and placing them in a large paper bag. She writes preparation instructions on the side of the bag—simple enough that even a non-cook like Raven can understand. Setting that aside, she fills an empty coffee can with the dried herbs for the healing tea—willow, chamomile, sweet grass, and dandelion to calm the system, stinging nettle and spiral orchid to purify the blood, and boneset for fever. In a Mason jar, she packs three long lengths of honeycomb full of honey for sweetening the tea.

Fawn takes the lid off a tiny pine straw basket and removes a dry grayish bundle of sage, wrapped with colored embroidery thread. She lights the tip, and then blows out the flame. Inhaling the smoke from the smoldering sage, she holds it in her lungs. She closes her eyes and asks Father Spirit to bless the tea, and then exhales the smoke into the canister, quickly sealing the medicine with the plastic lid. *It may save her life*, she confirms.

"I love the smell of sage," Dane says behind her. "It's one of the few things that doesn't interfere with my clairscent abilities."

Fawn gives him the basket, the paper bag, the coffee can, the jar, and a stern look. "Never forget the old ways, Dane. They've kept our people going for many years."

"Mmmmm! What's that?" Raven says.

"Sage. It cleanses your home, your body, and your mind. Dane can show you how to use it. If you run out, let me know, and I will send more…and *sofkee* and morning tea. These are things you must have," Fawn says. She reaches down beneath the table platform and retrieves a larger basket, this one made of split palm leaves. "In this basket are things I want you to have. When they heard Dane was getting married, all the ladies in the village made you something."

Raven removes the lid of the basket and pulls out the contents one by one. The first is a tiny box, no larger than a deck of cards, completely covered with seed beads. Inside, Raven finds a set of dangle earrings, a bracelet, and a matching triple strand necklace of red, yellow, white, and black seed beads offset with tiny porcupine quills.

"The jewelry is made by Mary Wilbur. She's the best jewelry maker in the village," Fawn says. "The metal is sterling silver, and the quills came from a porcupine in the woods behind the village." Seeing Raven's wide eyes, she laughs and says, "Oh, don't fret, Raven. She didn't kill him. She got them from her curious dog's nose. The beaded box is from Minnie Louie. She's a master in the folk life apprenticeship program."

Raven replaces the jewelry in the small box and reaches back into the basket. Wrapped in a piece of cloth are two dolls, about eighteen inches tall. The male doll is dressed in a long, belted shirt like the ones she saw in the gift shop. On its head is a cloth turban. It has no hands at the end of the long shirt sleeves, and the legs are bare, ending in an indication of moccasins. The eyes and mouth are very simply sewn in colored embroidery floss; the nose, a ridge pulled tightly with thread.

The female doll is dressed in a patchwork skirt and short shawl. It also has no hands, and the facial features are embroidered. Around its neck is a replica of Raven's necklaces, and identical earrings hang from a place where ears should be. The doll's hair is black cloth, fashioned to look like Fawn's "hair hat." Both dolls are made from a course fiber, giving them a dark reddish-brown skin color.

"Susie Osceola is our doll artist. She uses the traditional palmetto fiber for the bodies."

"I recognize my jewelry and your hair," Raven observes.

"That's right. It's a conspiracy. We all got together to make everything match up. Notice the patterns in your doll's dress. They each have special significance."

Raven looks closer at her doll. She points to each line of patchwork in turn as Fawn explains the symbols. The uppermost patchwork strip is brown with white symbols, each of which looks like upside down "T" with another white line extending from the juncture at an angle running southwest to northeast.

"That is your clan symbol. Dane says your clan is bird."

"Yes. That looks a little like a bird's foot."

The next strip shows a jagged white expanse above a jagged red expanse, giving the appearance of white teeth above blood red ones.

"That one is the symbol for fire," Fawn says.

"Oh. I thought it was teeth," Raven says.

"Fire has been known to bite, it's true, but focus on the red flames instead of the white part overhead. This symbolizes your mate. Since Dane is a fire marshal, we thought this pattern was appropriate. The next one below stands for the four directions—the medicine colors. Black diamonds in the north and south, red diamonds in the east and west, separated by the yellow cross, or 'X' mark, on a white background. This is for protection, health, and to help you find your way in all things."

"And the last pattern?" Raven asks, pointing to a black strip with white vertical lines, cut by two smaller horizontal lines in the upper half of the line.

"That is the symbol for tree—the way the love between you and your mate should grow."

Raven looks at the dolls in wonder, noticing similar patterns on the male doll's shirt. "I recognize fire, four directions, and tree. What's that one?" she says, indicating a pattern of alternating white and turquoise zig-zags running northwest to southeast on a black background.

"That is lightning—the symbol for power. Lightning is one of the strongest elements in the universe. It gives light and fire, life and death. Dane is the seventh son of a seventh son, and he holds power that has passed down through many generations. You must be a seventh child, too. Dane says you have the gift."

"I draw what is and isn't visible to the naked eye. Dane and the others are training me now. And let me tell you, it isn't as easy as I thought it would be!" Raven laments.

"Don't let her kid you, Mom. She's doing great,"

Dane says, winking at his sweetheart.

"Fawn. One thing I don't get. You said that Dane is the seventh son. That makes Noah the eighth. How did he get the gift?" Raven asks.

Fawn's smile freezes as she looks at Raven, and then at Dane. "That's a question we have been asked before. Noah would not ordinarily have the second-sight," she admits.

Raven looks at her to complete the explanation.

"Power is its own master; it touches those of its own choosing," Fawn says simply.

"What about you? Do you have the gift?"

"Power also chose me, but I am not gifted like you and the boys are. I learned my arts from my mother. She was Cedar Woman—a healer. And now I am Cedar Woman, too. But that's a story for another time. You have more presents. The last one I made myself."

Raven reaches into her basket now and pulls out a skirt and shawl identical to the one worn by her doll. She jumps to her feet holding the clothing up against her, swinging around so that the skirt fans out from her legs.

"Wow! This is gorgeous! I can't wait to wear it. But not today. It's too pretty for every day. I'm going to save it for a special occasion..." She stands very still and looks up at Fawn. "I'm going to save it for my wedding day, if that's alright with you."

Fawn rushes forward and squeezes the young

woman tightly in a fierce embrace. "That is the greatest gift you can ever give me, Raven. I am so honored."

Dane waits as long as he can to separate the two women, but he knows the time is short, and he and Raven need to return to Tallahassee. Work beckons, and the dead cannot rest until The Trackers discover the cause of their passing. Amid kisses and tears, they part ways.

CHAPTER EIGHT
IN SICKNESS

THE RETURN TRIP TO TALLAHASSEE passes much the same way as the trip to Tampa did. Raven naps most of the way, waking to guzzle Diet Coke and reapply her perfume. True to Dane's fear, the canister is emptied before they even get to the town of Perry. Raven mourns the end of her fragrance with atypical crankiness, complaining about the heat and the discomfort of the car seat. Dane pulls into a rest area, so she can walk and stretch her legs a bit. When she returns from the restroom, he suggests that she draw for a while.

"With what? On what?" she snaps.

Bringing his hands out from behind his back, he presents her with a box of sharpened colored pencils and a spiral-bound sketch pad. Instantly, her mood changes to childish delight.

"You are the best!" she exclaims.

"Mom's not the only Lightfoot around to bear

presents, m'love," he says.

Raven climbs in the seat and, after a thank-you kiss, flips the pad open on her lap.

"What'cha gonna draw?" he asks.

"Your mother," she says, busily sketching the face she sees so clearly in her mind. This is not only her gift, but her talent as well. She hums tunelessly while she draws.

Dane is pleased that she is distracted, at last. *I'll get a new canister of DeVanille for her just as soon as we get back to Tallahassee,* he decides. He glances over at her, and then he settles in for the remainder of the long drive.

Raven takes great care with the portrait of Fawn. She draws her profile, gazing wistfully off into the sky. But the finished picture seems sad, as if Fawn is looking for something she cannot find. That is not the way Raven wants to draw her, but *the pencil is its own master.* She cocks her head to the side. *Funny. That's what Fawn said about Power.*

She flips to the next page and begins again. She decides to sketch a frontal head shot. The image she creates is wonderful. It captures the exquisite lines of Fawn's face and the ubiquitous "hair hat." As she adds contours, color, and shading, it appears that Fawn is right there looking at her. She finishes the picture and looks away out the window.

When she looks back at the image, she is aware that something is not quite right. She studies the face and finds the flaw. The eyes. The eyes are the right shape but the wrong color. Fawn has black onyx eyes in her honey-colored face. The eyes in Raven's picture are light blue—almost silver. The sight of them sends a cramp to her stomach. *I know these eyes—don't I?*

Irritated, she flips to yet another page. This time she draws a full-length picture of Fawn with her hand on the head of her pet goose, Emma. *Oh, yes. This one is going to be special.* Fawn is looking down toward the goose, and she wears a tender smile on her lips. The goose has its head lifted toward the woman, its golden eye shining. Fawn wears her traditional Seminole skirt and shawl, dangling earrings, and seed bead necklaces, and her hair is twisted into a long braid which hangs over her shoulder. Her feet are bare on the swept dirt floor of her *chickee*, and in her other hand she holds the smoldering stick of sage. This is the Fawn she met at the Seminole Village. This is the mother-in-law she already loves.

Satisfied at last, Raven finishes her portrait of Fawn and flips the page over to the next blank. She stares at the paper for a while, waiting for an image to form in her mind. Her vision blurs, and she begins to draw. Her hand moves rapidly and jerkily across the page, and an animal theme emerges. She draws a striped and spotted cat with an elongated muzzle. It stands inside a small cage, its paw lifted, its lips pulled back in a hiss. A tiny long-handled spoon rests in the foreground. Over and over the motif repeats—cat, cage, spoon, cat, cage, spoon. Suddenly she stiffens and moans, "get me…get me…ho….home."

Dane hears Raven moan and looks at her in alarm. Seeing her stiff posture and closed eyes, he recognizes that she has fallen into a trance. He pulls the car over to the shoulder of the road and closes his eyes, sending a homing beacon for her to follow. In a minute, she opens her eyes to find him staring at her.

"Babe...you were tracking. Are you O.K.?"

"Yeah, I'm fine. I didn't mean to track, Dane. Sheesh! What's wrong with me?" Looking down at the paper in her hands, she gives it her complete attention. "Look at this! What in the world? I can draw better than this."

"Um...is that a cat? With a really long nose?"

"I don't know what it is. And what does a spoon have to do with a cat? I'm losing it, Dane. I think I'm coming down with the flu or something."

"What feels bad? Do you have to throw up?"

"No, but I ache all over, my throat is so dry, I'm burning up...and I can't go."

"What are you saying?"

"I keep going into the restrooms, but I can't seem to go. I can't pee!" She gasps, gulping for air. "I'm sick, honey. I'm really sick. Please get me home."

"We're almost there, Babe. Just hang on." Jamming on the accelerator, he fishtails onto the blacktop. Ignoring the unwritten five-miles-over-the-speed-limit rule, he races down the highway, passing cars left and right. Up ahead, he sees the exit that takes them to his house, but looking over at the misery Raven is in, he decides to bypass the turnoff and head to Tallahassee Memorial Hospital. *Mom was right; she is more than sick.*

Dane pulls the car up to the curb of the emergency entrance, slams it into park, and rushes around the front to open Raven's door. Gathering her in his arms, he carries her inside and up to the desk. Raven is in respiratory distress, so they take her in to a treatment room immediately.

Dane paces in the waiting room, aware that his true love's life hangs on the abilities of the doctors to heal her. Waiting is torture, but waiting alone is worse than torture, so he uses the desk phone to call Lee, asking him to pass the call along to Noah and Graham.

Less than 15 minutes later, Lee arrives, followed by Noah and Graham.

"Dane, what happened?" Lee asks, hurrying up to the younger man.

"I don't know, Hona. She started getting wiggy on the way home. Then she tracked while she was asleep. After that, it was downhill, and I knew she was in a pretty bad way."

"She tracked?" Lee asks.

"Yeah. Not intentionally. More like she went into a trance. She drew the most gosh-awful picture of a cat. Well, it sorta looked like a cat—a mutated one. I don't know. It was weird. Then, right after that, she got really, really ill," Dane says.

"What do you think is going on?" Noah asks.

"Noah, Mom said Raven was sick. No, Mom said Raven was poisoned. I don't know how that can be, but I think she was right."

"You know Mom. She knows those things. We have to figure out what poisoned her."

"Sure, don't worry, Dane. We'll find out who or what did this to her," Graham says.

Dane walks to the water fountain and spots the doctor. He sprints over to the door, just as the man enters the waiting room.

"Doctor—uh—Vidjapore, is she O.K.?" Dane asks.

"She will be fine, but I am keeping her for a few days to force fluids and get her temperature down. A high fever is especially dangerous, given her condition," he says gruffly in impeccably accented King's English.

Dane's eyes widen. "Is the…I mean, will she…what about the…"

"You should have thought about that before now, but, yes, everything is all right, so far," he huffs.

His manner puzzles the men waiting in the room. The doctor seems almost angry.

Lee walks up beside Dane. "Doctor, can you tell us what happened to her?"

"Who might you be, her father?" the doctor asks.

"No, I am her friend. This is her fiancé. We are quite worried about her. Perhaps you can explain her condition,"

Lee says evenly.

"Well, she is very lucky you brought her to the hospital. She is terribly dehydrated, her kidneys have been compromised, and she is on the verge of hypterthermia," he reports.

"What? Like getting frostbite?" Noah asks.

"No, it is the opposite. You are thinking of hypothermia. This girl is quite severely overheated," the doctor says.

"That sounds like ecstasy!" Dane says.

"Yes, young man. You are fortunate she is not dead. She has a considerable quantity of gamma hydroxybutyric acid in her bloodstream. You young people may think that ecstasy is fun and makes your relationship sexier, but it is a dangerous substance," the doctor admonishes. "In large doses, the drug can cause complete system breakdown. Your young lady is seriously ill."

"Whoa, whoa. Wait a minute. We have not taken ecstasy. In fact, we are working with the police department investigating ecstasy-related deaths," Dane insists.

Lee steps forward and puts his hand on Dane's shoulder, glancing back at Noah, who has a reputation for speaking and acting with thinking first. Graham takes the hint and pushes in closer to the young hothead.

"Doctor Vidjapore, we think that someone has been introducing an ecstasy drug into common foods or drinks, and people are having reactions to it. You can check with

Chief Rowan of the Tampa Police Department. We've just come from there," Dane explains.

"Yeah, we aren't dope-heads," Noah growls.

"You may also contact Chief Jack Abernathy of the Tallahassee Police Department to confirm, Doctor," Lee says with a restrained tone.

Doctor Anjul Vidjapore, a naturalized Indian American, appraises the Native Americans in his waiting room and realizes that he has committed an act he has fought to overcome since he first immigrated to the United States from Bombay. He has judged them on the basis of their ethnic origins, and he is ashamed.

"Please accept my sincerest apologies, gentlemen. I see so many people in here who have abused the social drugs that I jumped to conclusions. But the fact remains, the young lady is suffering from ecstasy poisoning—much like a teenage boy and girl I tried to revive just last week. Those kids died, but your lady will recover," he says humbly.

"Thank you, sir," Lee says. "We appreciate your candor. Perhaps we may work together to solve this crisis affecting our young people."

"Can I...can I see her?" Dane asks anxiously.

"Of course, you can. We are not overly busy tonight. We have already been able to move her to a room. You may all go in, if you wish. But try not to overwhelm her. Her condition is fragile, and I have given her a sedative, so she will rest," Doctor Vidjapore says.

The Trackers follow the doctor's directions to Raven's room and stand before the partially closed door, unsure of what to do next. Finally, Noah pushes his way to the front and enters the room, the others following behind him.

Raven lies in the bed, an IV running from her forearm to a bag of clear saline solution overhead. She is pale, and her hair is splayed out on the pillow. Her breathing is shallow, but regular. A white sheet and cotton blanket cover her thin frame.

Dane sits on the rolling stool and walks it to her side, holding her hand. Noah moves to the other side, examining the IV bag, the blood pressure cuff, and everything else in the room. Lee and Graham stand guard at the foot rail. Nobody speaks. They just stare at her, willing her to be well.

A tiny line of spittle escapes the side of Raven's mouth, and Dane reaches forward to wipe it away. She wakes and regards the somber faces assembled around her bed. She tries to speak, but her throat is dry. On a nearby wheeled table is a pink cup full of ice chips. She nods in the direction of the tray. Dane grabs the cup and gives her a spoonful of chips. She rolls them around in her mouth, sucking the melting water down her parched throat.

She smiles wanly, clears her throat, and utters one word, "bleep."

CHAPTER NINE
TRACKING THE DRUG

THE EMERGENCY CRISIS WITH RAVEN has the entire Trackers Team unnerved. It is one thing to track strangers and casual acquaintances, but it is another when one of the team is compromised. Now, it has become a personal case. Even though it is late, the men gather at Dane's house to discuss a plan of action, and an argument inevitably ensues.

"No, Graham. She's my fiancé, I'm tracking," Dane insists, clenching his fists.

"Lightfoot, you are the most stubborn man I have ever known," Graham scowls.

"Guilty as charged."

"Except for your squirrely little brother, that is."

"Ditto," Noah says.

"Gentlemen!" Lee says. "I have heard enough squabbling. I am pulling rank here. Dane, you make the first track. Sniff out the scent you picked up at the night club and compare it to whatever you can smell at Marjorie Collier's home. Noah will beacon for you. Then I want you, Graham, to track to the same nightclub and listen for any references to ecstasy or illegal drug activity. I will beacon for you. Does everybody understand? Under no circumstances are the four of us to be traveling or beaconing at the same time."

Ever since Noah was abducted, leaving Lee without a beacon, this had been a hard and fast rule. At least one person must be fully aware at all times.

All the men nod in agreement. Dane and Noah face each other across the table, while Graham and Lee seat themselves on the couch to wait. In just a short time, the Lightfoot boys are breathing in sync.

In less than ten minutes, Dane returns from his track looking confused and frustrated.

"Nothing. I can't smell anything but sweat and body odor and old flowers at the club tonight. The scent I tracked that first night was heavy and cloying, like rotted oranges covered with mold. And sort of like a damp locker room. You know—musty, or musky, I guess. I can still smell a little bit of the oranges. It's faint, but it's all over the room."

"What about Marjorie Collier?" Graham asks.

"Same thing. Nothing really jumps out at me. But, then, her place is like going into the mall during Christmas. All the women at the cosmetics counters are spritzing you with perfume samples. Makes me gag."

"It's my turn, then," Graham says. "I'm going

clubbing!" He closes his eyes and begins tracking. As his beacon, Lee closes his eyes in turn and listens for the word.

Graham's track is also short—fifteen minutes in all. When he returns and opens his eyes, the team is waiting anxiously for his report. Taking a deep breath, Graham begins speaking in the voices of the people he has just heard.

"Hey, man. I'm looking to score some happy. Got any?" a young man asks, his voice a tremulous tenor.

"Depends on what you're looking for, pal," a deeper baritone-voiced young man says.

"I need Kleenex—for my runny nose. You dig?" the tenor voice says.

"Sorry, but 'The Mister' is already gone," the deep baritone voice says.

"Maaan!" the tenor whines. "When's 'The Master' coming back?

The baritone snickers. "He's not the 'Master,' you dweeb. It's 'Mister,' and he won't be back until next week."

The tenor curses. "This kills my buzz. My girl's gonna freak. I promised her I'd X her tonight! Now what am I gonna do?"

"Hey there, handsome. 'The Mister' left some scent samples with me, if you want to surprise her with a tester," a female with a lilting soprano voice says.

"And what's a tester, sweet thing?" the tenor asks.

"All the latest fragrances in spray testers. I've got the perfumes in my bag, but they aren't cheap," the soprano says.

"Why would I want a perfume?" the tenor asks.

"Because 'The Mister' has added some special ingredients to them. And each one comes with a lollipop of your choice," the soprano croons.

"What about X?" the tenor asks.

"Um hm. I bet your girl would like *Chatoyant No. 2* or maybe *VinDoux*," the soprano says.

"*Chatoyant* for sure. How much?" the tenor asks.

"Two bills for a guaranteed rush like you've never known. Your girl will really thank you—if you know what I mean," the soprano says.

"Give me both," the tenor says. "I'll have two chances at heaven."

Graham stops talking and looks around at his stunned team mates. Each is lost in his own thoughts; the news is more horrific than they even imagined.

Lee breaks the silence. "Tainted perfumes full of narcotics. What kind of person would even dream of doing such a thing?"

Dane bites his lower lip and stares at the floor. Noah reaches over and places his hand on his brother's shoulder, noticing that giant tears are landing on Dane's knees behind the curtain of his long black hair.

"I poisoned her. It was in her perfume all the time, and I didn't even know," he whispers.

"Dane, it has no scent. There was no way you

could've picked it up. You couldn't know her perfume was laced with drugs."

"I should have known. Mom was right. Raven was poisoned from the inside. It went through her skin, Noah. Through her skin and into her bloodstream. I almost killed her!" He puts his head in his hands and weeps bitterly.

Noah embraces his stricken brother, not even bothering to stem his own tears. Lee and Graham move back, letting the brothers console each other.

"What do you think, Graham? Is this 'Mister' a local man, or could he be from out of town? Tampa, perhaps?" Lee says.

"I'm betting he is from a larger city. Could be Tampa. I don't really know. I couldn't get a sense of his location from my track. That's your specialty. Let's give the boys a little time to get themselves together and then see if you can track him," Graham says.

"I'm O.K. Find this guy, Lee. You track him, and I'll go get him," Dane says. His face is damp, and his eyes are swollen, but his demeanor is hard. "I'll beacon."

"No, Dane. You and Noah take notes. You are much too emotional to beacon for me right now. Graham will do it. Go to the table and take notes. I will find him," Lee says.

Dane nods jerkily, knowing that his friend is right. Noah is already at the table with pencil and paper. He pushes a piece to his brother's seat. Pencils in hand, they watch as Lee and Graham settle onto the couch. In just a few minutes, Lee sighs. Eyes closed tightly in his trance, he begins to talk, and the two Lightfoot boys begin transcribing his track.

"His steed is black as night, a fearsome cat poised to run. It races north, eyes blazing, reflecting the white and yellow stripes before its paws. It is dark as pitch and cold...colder...colder. The ground is brown, dead, covered with crystals. Red and yellow leaves fly away as he passes by. He has run for a long, long time. The sun set hours ago, and the moon is high to his right, and yet he races on and on," Lee intones. He is quiet for a short time, and then he begins speaking again.

"He slows now, his journey nearly ending. The stars before him are everywhere. High, low, right, left. Their colors shimmer and sparkle in circles, rectangles, dancing lines. He rests beneath the bright and brilliant spirits, amid the pulsing stars all around, near the wooded park in the center of the apple. And the Tracker now comes home," Lee says, opening his eyes.

Noah and Dane are already looking at their notes, deciphering the clues that Lee has given them through his poetic metaphor.

"What'd he say, guys?" Graham asks.

"See for yourself. This is one quirky poem this time!" Noah says.

"I got the car, I think," Dane says. "It's definitely black, and I think it's a Jag. That's the only 'cat' car that I know of."

"I'm with you there," Noah says. "Jaguars have that neat silver figurine on the hood—the cat poised to run."

"Going north, eyes blazing—that's headlights for sure. Reflecting white and yellow stripes on the road," Graham says, looking over Dane's shoulder.

"It's getting colder as he goes farther north. Leaves falling, frost on the ground. Way farther north," Dane says.

"He left before sunset, and it's taking a long time because it's night, and the moon is high," Noah says, checking his notes.

"Still going north. Moon's up in the east, on the right side of the car," Dane agrees.

"Where's he stopped?" Graham asks.

"Stars all around. Colors, shapes, dancing?" Dane says, eyes wide.

"Neon! Big city lights. Signs. He's in a large city in a downtown area," Noah says.

"Good catch, little bro," Dane says.

"A big city with a wooded park in the center of the apples? Wooded park. Apple trees?" Graham says.

"No, he said 'apple'—singular," Dane says.

"Woodville, Longwood, Parker, Applewood. I can't think of any big cities with wood, park, or apple in their names," Noah says, chewing on his pencil.

"Central Park," Lee says. "It is in the…"

"Big Apple!" the men say in unison.

"He's in New York City," Dane says.

"Exactly," Lee says.

"And that's where I'm going," Dane says, jumping up to grab his coat.

"Not without me, you don't," Noah says, knocking his chair over in his haste to get up.

"Just one minute, you two," Lee says. "Nobody is going anywhere without a plan of action. It is so like you boys to run off half-cocked like this. Dane. Noah. Sit! Now. There is plenty of time to go hunting, but let's know what we're dealing with before you go. Sit, I said."

Like chastised children, Dane and Noah plop down on the couch while Lee casually picks up the telephone and dials Jack Abernathy's home number.

"He's right, you know," Noah says. "We don't even know who we're looking for."

"Someone called 'Mister,' which could be just about anyone," Graham says.

"You said, '*The* Mister,' Gray. That's a little more specific," Noah points out.

"I stand corrected, but that doesn't change the fact that none of us have seen his face or even heard his voice. We need a little more info from Chief Abernathy," Graham says, shrugging his broad shoulders.

"Aaaaagh! You're right. I'm just so…" Dane says.

"…impulsive…insane?" Graham offers.

"Oh, step off, Gray," Dane says.

"Step off? Did you really just say, 'step off?' You've been watching *Seinfeld* again!" This sends Graham into a giggling fit that passes to the other men when he starts doing impressions of the characters from the TV sitcom. The tension broken by much needed laughter, they all relax and wait for Lee to finish gathering information from the Police Chief.

Lee hangs up the phone and takes a seat at the table. "Jack is checking on the man called 'The Mister' from the club. And he is dispatching a detail to the club to find the girl with the perfume testers. Graham, you may have to go to the station and do a voice I.D. tonight. Is that alright with you?" Lee says.

"Sure thing. I can identify the bartender and the other guy, too, if they round everybody up and if the guy and his girl are still there," Graham says.

"What about us finding this guy in New York?" Dane asks. "That is going to be a little tricky since we do not know anything about him. Jack can coordinate with the NYPD to see if there have been any ecstasy-related deaths up there involving tainted perfumes," Lee says.

"I'm still going, Hona. Remember the moldy orange smell I told you about. I know what it is. It's a sickness smell. Jimbo had that smell. I don't know why I didn't recognize it before. Guess I blocked it out," Dane says.

"Jimbo had cancer, Dane. You can smell cancer? Impressive," Noah says.

"I suppose. Anyhow, I'm sure it's the guy. He's covered in the perfume scents, but there's that underlying odor of disease. That's what I've been trying to identify. It was on the kids at the club and the Collier woman...and on Raven. It wasn't the ecstasy—it was the man. He touched the bottles. If I can smell him, I can find him!" Dane insists.

"And if he's going, I'm going," Noah says. "Your rule—nobody tracks alone."

"Fine," Lee says. "You are both going—in the morning! Tonight, you two must get some sleep. Graham and I will work things from this end, along with Jack. Pack warm clothes, boys. New York is a very cold city, in more ways than just the weather."

CHAPTER TEN
COUNTRY BOYS IN THE CITY

LEE IS RIGHT ABOUT NEW YORK. It is a very cold city, in many ways. For two young men born and raised in balmy Florida, the temperature difference is extreme, and so is the culture shock. As soon as they step out of the airport at LaGuardia, the Lightfoots know they are in a foreign land.

The taxi ride to the city is less than pleasant, and they are sure that they will die in a horrible traffic accident. The driver speaks a form of English that neither of them can understand, and the fare is more than they anticipated. Fortunately, Lee had the foresight to give them plenty of cash and his own credit card. They lug their bags out of the trunk, thankful to be alive as the car careens back into the sea of vehicles.

After checking into their hotel, Dane and Noah hit the streets to find the New York Police Department. They decide that walking may be the safer option, so armed with a map of the city and a subway schedule, they exit the hotel and survey the alien surroundings.

Gone are the large expanses of grassy lawns in front of wood framed houses with screened-in porches. Instead, there are endless concrete sidewalks leading to row upon row of apartment buildings, their cracked cement steps framed with iron handrails and heavy front doors covered over in years of reapplied paint. There are no flowers, no yard gnomes, no dog houses in sight. The few trees are segregated by spindly wrought-iron fences surrounding their meager trunks, which jut out from between the sidewalk sections.

Looking up, the gray sky peeks between towering buildings with metal staircases running like rick-rack to the roofs. As the clouds move overhead, Noah's sense of balance is confounded. He grips the handrail to steady himself and vows not to look up ever again. Instead, he studies the undulating crowd of bodies.

The people walk with purpose, not stopping to chat or visit with neighbors. Nobody saunters, nobody lopes. Their gate is brisker than the weather. Wrapped in long coats, scarves around their necks, hats on their heads, gloves on their hands, they seem like a marching army advancing on the enemy. They push, they shove, they elbow. They just keep going.

And then there is the smell. Dane spends much of the time shielding his nose from the onslaught of odors. The best scents are those of baking bread, roasting meats, and foods of every ethnic origin. The worst are the stench of the unwashed, the vehicle exhausts, and the combined mix of the expensive fragrances worn by virtually every moving ant in the colony. But of all the odors, Dane's scent identification of New York City is that of roasting chestnuts and urine.

For Noah, the sight of so much activity makes his eyes hurt. He can't stop looking. The movement on the street draws his attention like moving strings draw cats. And as he looks, his eidetic mind stores and catalogs the information until it seems his head will burst. His only solution is to look directly at the ground, at the forward motion of his own two feet, while he presses close to his brother.

Thankfully, the New York Police Department is just up ahead. He relies on Dane to lead the way, relieved when they ascend the stairs and enter the front doors. But, looking up, he realizes that the hubbub continues inside the building. He spots a clock and fixes his gaze on that one solitary object.

The desk Sergeant is a slender, middle-aged man, with short brown hair and a small mustache. He looks nothing like the television cop stereotype. And, in contrast to their expectations, he is polite and helpful, directing them to an office for a meeting with a detective familiar with their agenda. Once again, Lee and Jack have already paved the way for them.

Detective Michael Ortega shakes their hands and

offers them seats across from his desk. He smiles often and has a habit of running his long fingers through his thinning hair. Dane and Noah feel comfortable with him at once.

"We got a call from your Chief Abernathy late last night and were able to pull quite a lot of information about the notorious perp in question. He's called 'The Mister' because of the way he traffics illegal narcotics. In perfumes, of all things. He adds GHB—liquid X—to the perfumes and sells them in their original bottles. They call him 'The Mister' because all the products he moves have spray bulbs or push down atomizers. The drug gets in the system through the skin, and sometimes by inhaling the fine mist. It's hard to detect because ecstasy has no distinguishable odor. It doesn't interfere with the smell of the fragrance," Chief Ortega says.

"Yeah. We found that out," Noah says. "You can't tell if a bottle is tainted or not."

"That's what makes it so hard to catch this guy. You should know that New York has a huge counterfeit fragrance ring, and we can't seem to bust it up. We've had undercover working it for years. Every time we catch a break, another boss takes over and sets up in a different location. We think 'The Mister' was part of this ring, but not anymore. In fact, we think he's gone solo with his own special brand of counterfeiting and tampering. The kids love it because their parents can't tell they're tripping. The laced testers are easier to get their hands on, cheaper, and can be concealed in a purse or a pocket," Ortega says.

Or a moccasin, Dane thinks.

"We've found ecstasy in perfumes as far south as Tampa," Noah says.

"Yeah. We think he's running a line from New York to Tampa and possibly points in between. But mostly in Florida. I think that's where he's establishing his territory. You've discovered three deaths?" Ortega says.

"That's all we know of for now. There could be more, but we haven't been on the case very long," Dane says.

"I understand. And how did you discover the 'smellex' was the cause?" Ortega asks.

"What did you just say?" Noah asks.

Ortega smiles and shrugs. "We call it 'smellex' here. You know—smell ecstasy," he says. "Everything has a nickname on the streets."

"Uh huh. Well, my fiancé got terribly sick from it," Dane says.

"Really? How'd she get hold of it?" Ortega asks.

"I bought it from a small boutique in Tallahassee," Dane says. "I didn't know it was laced, and I bet they didn't either. Do you think that guy has a partner? So far, the other victims bought it at a club,"

"No, Dane. What about Marjorie Collier? I bet she didn't get it at a club. She seemed to be wealthy," Noah says

"The wealthy like a good deal as well as the lower class," Ortega says. "Need to check out that boutique. See if it's a chain or franchise or a personally-owned small business."

"Right. I'll have Lee get on it," Noah says.

"What can you tell me about this 'Mister' character? All we know for sure is that he frequents the clubs in Florida and drives a black jaguar," Dane says.

"No kidding? How'd you boys find that out?" Ortega asks, eyebrows raised.

Dane and Noah exchange glances. "Through our investigation. From—uh—a person at a club who saw a guy drive away in a fancy car," Noah says.

"Good work. That's more than we have. Here, he's in the shadows. In the wind. We don't know what he looks like. Nobody has him on the radar, as far as I know, in New York. But we're sure he gets his product here," Ortega says.

"Do you have any idea where? Is it a major fragrance manufacturing house?" Noah asks.

"The perfume I got for my fiancé was a major brand, from Guerlain. I know they are based here in New York," Dane says.

"Look, you guys. I'm all for helping out other departments, but I'm not comfortable with you two nosing around where you don't belong. No offense or anything, but you're not cops. Abnernathy said to give you information. That's it. I don't want you Florida guys turning up dead in my town," Ortega says.

For once, Noah is the level-headed brother. He grasps Dane's forearm and settles him before he can jump up. "We understand, sir. We are just investigating and trying to get a handle on what we're dealing with in Florida. If you can give us any leads that we can take back with us, we really appreciate it."

"No problem. I'm not trying to be a jerk. It's just that you guys could get hurt, you know. I'll make you a copy of the file pertaining to 'The Mister' for your Chief. And if you want to know more about how they make perfumes, check out the Fashion Institute of Technology. They started the Fragrance Foundation. My wife and I visited once. It's an interesting place, but too foo-foo for my taste." Ortega wrinkles his nose.

"Thanks. That sounds like a plan. We'll go there before we leave for home," Noah says.

Michael Ortega takes the file and leaves the office to make a copy. Dane turns angrily to Noah. "I'm not going home until I find this guy," he growls.

"Me neither, bro. But I'm not telling that detective. Let's just go along with him thinking we're gonna sightsee a little before we leave. I sure don't want to tick him off and be made to go back before we're ready."

Dane presses his lips together and nods, patting Noah on the shoulder. In just a moment, Ortega returns with a stack of stapled papers. He smiles and remains standing, the cue for the men to end their meeting.

"Thanks again, Detective Ortega. You've been a great help," Dane says.

"No problem. I hope you catch him in Florida and

save me the paperwork," he says.

"Yeah, I gotcha. Oh, by the way. We heard that he gives out lollipops with his spray testers. What's up with that?" Noah says.

"That's for the 'clamping' side effect. X users tend to clench their jaws and grind their teeth. Sucking lollipops is one way to relieve that tendency. Also, you might see them wearing big baby pacifiers around their necks for the same reason. The clubs around here keep bubble gum and suckers on the bar. As far as dope goes, ecstasy is one of the milder ones, but deadly just the same."

A chill races down Dane's back as he thinks back to Raven chewing pack after pack of gum. *If I'd only known*, he laments.

"Good luck," Ortega says. "Hope you enjoy the tour. Don't buy any perfume while you're here, though. You'll go broke."

Noah and Dane laugh and make their way out to the street and the pandemonium that is New York City. Consulting their map, they locate the street address for the Fashion Institute of Technology, and it necessitates another harrowing taxi ride. This time, their driver is a young Jamaican man with a huge colorful cap of green, orange, and purple barely containing the dreadlocks inside it and a gold front tooth that gleams when he smiles—which he does frequently. Unlike the other cabbie, Jaffey—which he pronounces "jah-Fee"—is chatty and personable.

"You visitin' te city, eh? For te first time, Mon?"

Jaffey says to the older Lightfoot brother.

"Yep. First time. Y'all sure have a lot of people."

"Who is Joll?"

"No, not joll—y'all. It's short for you all."

"Oh, you are from te south? Jaffey know te south. Grits and hounddogs and tings like tat. Tis warm down in te south, eh?"

"By comparison, yeah. Hey Jaffey, what do you know about street dope sold in perfume?" Noah asks.

"You tink all Jamaicans are dopeheads? Jaffey does not take dope. If tat is what you are here for, you get out of tis cab," Jaffey says frowning.

"No, no, no. You misunderstand. We're working with the police from down in Florida," Dane says.

"My brother's fiancé was given some perfume laced with ecstasy, and she's very sick. We're trying to find out where it came from," Noah says.

"If you are narco, ten you better be careful. Te X trafficers are very bad, Mon. Tey will kill you if you cross tem. Don't go talkin' like tis to jus anybody. You already look different, you know!"

"We look different?"

"Yes. Wit tat long black hair and tem dark tans. You 'tract attention. Good lookin' Indian fellows, too. Be careful. Bad people here."

"Thanks, Man. Appreciate the heads up," Dane says to the cabbie.

"Hey, Jaffey. Did you know that your name means

'trickster rabbit' in our language?" Noah says.

"Is tat right?" Jaffey laughs, a deep resonant sound from his chest, before pulling his cab to a stop at the curb.

"Yeah, except we spell it c-v-f-e. Still pronounced 'Cha- Fee' though."

"Hmm. Maybe it would be good to change te spelling. Jaffey might be a trickster, eh? Here is te place you are going. And here is my card. If you get into any trouble— and Jaffey is afraid tat you might—call tat number and Jaffey will come get you. Keep your money. Jaffey is a big fan of te Seminoles." Jaffey pulls his cab back into the flow of traffic, but Dane and Noah can still hear him singing the Seminole war chant.

In front of them stands the Fashion Institute of Technology—a mid-century structure of metal panels in a harlequin pattern. Inside they hope to find some answers to the counterfeit perfume trade. They nod to each other and begin to climb the stairs. Before they reach the door, a young woman in garish pink fake fur thrusts a pamphlet into their hands.

"Save the civets," she says. "No more testing on innocent animals."

"Right on," says Noah, pumping his fist as he walks on past her.

Dane takes the literature and stuffs it in his back pocket. Together, he and Noah enter the front door, away from the visual and olfactory sensory overload of the streets.

CHAPTER ELEVEN
MAKING SCENTS

INSIDE THE FOYER OF THE INSTITUTE'S C building, also called the Martin Feldman Center, stands a mock-up of the plans for an expansion to the building, boasting Italian marble tile floors and spotless mirrors on the walls. Glassed-in staircases will flow like rivers all around the interior of the building, inspired by stitching patterns and folded fabric. A North Quad on the fifth-floor will allow direct accessibility to the C Building's South Quad, with glass expanses replacing an existing brick wall. It looks elegant and costly.

"Wow," Noah says. "And I thought F.S.U. was beautiful." Turning back, he notices that Dane is already at the desk, asking questions.

The petite blond receptionist pushes some leaflets across the desk with bright fuchsia manicured fingernails, letting her hand rest on the papers as he tries to pick them up. She stares boldly into Dane's eyes while tapping on the paper in his hand. He looks off to the right, and then back to Noah. He grins and thanks the coquette, not missing the wink of her heavily shadowed eye. Dane hurries to Noah's side, clutching the mass of handouts.

"Gag. I swear I can taste her cologne," Dane says rubbing his nose vigorously.

"Growl, meow, meow," Noah purrs.

"Scary. I thought she was going to pounce on me right there."

"Me, too. What'd you get?"

"Nobody here to talk to, but she said we can audit a class down the hall about Michael Edwards and the Fragrance Wheel."

"Who's that?"

"Beats me, but Francine said the class is a 'must go' for fragrance majors."

"Oooo. Francine, huh?"

"Shut up, you doofus. Let's go catch that class and see if we can learn something." Dane heads down the hall.

The double doors to the lecture hall squeak slightly as Dane opens them, and the two brothers wince as they tip toe into the room. Sliding into a couple of seats in the back row, they blink, adjusting their eyes to the darkness. In the front of the room, a large screen is filled with the image of a color wheel, of sorts. Dane counts thirteen different colors around the perimeter of the circle ranging from yellow to blue to green to a variety of pink and red hues. Around the colors are four different word groups categorizing floral notes, oriental notes, woody notes, and fresh notes. At the microphone, the speaker continues her lecture.

"...then, in 1983, Michael Edwards, a European perfumer, attended a fragrance seminar held by one of the largest privately-owned companies in the perfume business. Mr. Edwards was so inspired by the techniques he learned there that he developed the Fragrance Wheel you see pictured here. Edwards had been Halston's international fragrance director for some time until Halston retired and sold his company.

Edwards then moved to Sydney, Australia, to test market his scent guide. He *completely* revolutionized the fragrance industry when he developed his classification wheel. It took the *'perfumespeak'* out of selecting new fragrances. It takes accords, which you have learned are the foundation stones and base themes of raw material blends, and breaks them down into schemes, showing the relationships between each individual fragrance family. Since 1984, his guide for retailers has become *the* world's most comprehensive fragrance manual. It is updated annually to include all of the *Fragrances of the World."*

The screen image changes to that of a distinguished square-jawed man surrounded by perfume bottles of all shapes and sizes. The lecturer continues.

"Michael Edwards was *truly* a pioneer in the field of fragrances. I consider him a veritable spiritual figure, of sorts. He tells us the Koran states that 'perfumes are foods that reawaken the spirit.'

In his own words, Edwards says that his book is 'a fragrance map to a world of olfactory delights. A great perfume is a work of art. It is silent poetry, invisible body language. It can lift our days, enrich our nights and create the milestones of our memories. Fragrance is liquid emotion.'

The man is *simply genius!* Thank you for your attention. Class is dismissed."

Students begin leaving the room from doors on the sides and in the back. Dane and Noah find themselves swimming upstream in a river of people as they struggle to reach the lecturer. The woman looks up at them, startled by their appearance, as they introduce themselves.

"We are investigating some deaths in Florida from tainted perfumes, and we were hoping to learn a little about the industry while we are here," Dane says.

"Oh. That's terrible. Well, it didn't happen at this school," the instructor says.

"We weren't suggesting that it did. We, uh, just are wondering how somebody would go about putting an illegal substance in a perfume bottle. A spray bottle," Noah says.

"I'm not really sure that I can help you with that. We just teach the mechanics of fragrance combination, how to be an evaluator trainee, a fragrance architect, a nose..." she says.

"A nose?" Dane says.

She laughs a little, but not much. "A nose is a person with a *highly* developed sense of smell who identifies the elements in a perfume."

"Like on the wheel?"

"Exactly. I see you paid attention to my lecture." She seems pleased.

"Fascinating stuff. Edwards was a real pioneer."

"You really seem to have a good grasp of the industry, young man. Are you interested in becoming a perfumer?"

"Not me. But my brother—he's really got a good nose."

"Is that right? Let's test it, shall we? Can you tell what I am wearing?" she asks Dane.

Dane is up to the challenge. He leans closer to the woman and inhales deeply.

"Could you put the slide of the wheel back up, please?" he asks.

The professor obliges him, smirking slightly.

"O.K. Let's see. You are wearing, um, floral notes of jasmine…iris…white roses…lavender…daffodil…and some other flower I can't really identify," he says.

Her mouth hangs open, and then she purses her lips. "Very, *very* good. Lily of the valley. That's the one you missed. And the fixative?"

"I don't know what a fixative is," Dane admits.

"A fixative is the base note that holds the fragrances together and gives the scent longevity. It reduces the evaporation rate and improves stability, so the perfume keeps its original fragrance longer. The fixative of *my* perfume is amber. It's *quite* expensive."

"Amber is like a gemstone," Noah says.

"Amber is short for ambergris," she says.

"From whales?"

"Yes. The majority of base note fixatives are animal-based."

"Is that why the animal protection people are at your door?" Dane asks.

"Nuisances. Perfumers don't really harm animals," she huffs. "Nonetheless, I *am* impressed with your ability. Have you ever considered becoming a fragrance architect?"

"No, not really," he says. "I prefer fighting crime."

"Pity. Well, like I said, I can't really help you, but you might try the Sense of Smell Institute. They're the research end of the perfume industry. Good luck." She gathers her papers and flicks off the projector.

"Thanks for your help," Dane says, but she is already walking away.

"Hey!" Noah calls, causing her to turn back. "What's the name of your perfume?"

"*Les Fleurs du Peintre Français,*" she says before disappearing out the door.

"*The Flowers of the French Painter?* What a stupid

name. C'mon 'Nose,' let's go," Noah says clapping Dane on the back. They exit the building laughing.

The Sense of Smell Institute is a short walk away, so the two of them amble down the crowded sidewalk, shoving and bumping with the rest of the New York City population. After a brisk trek across the center of the city, they find themselves at the research facility. In contrast to the Fashion Institute, this place is more utilitarian. The men are instantly more comfortable.

The receptionist seems like a normal person. To Dane's relief, she doesn't try to hit on him. Also, he notices that the building has a rather neutral smell, and he is glad. The amalgamation of conflicting scents of the city have given him a pounding headache.

In a couple of minutes, a technician arrives wearing a plain white lab coat. The man is short and balding, but very obliging. He leads the men through a maze of hallways and into a spotless laboratory full of bottles, beakers, test tubes, and other technicians who smile at the sight of the handsome Native Americans in the lab.

"We are delighted to be of help to the police anytime we can. And especially to Florida police. I went there when I was a little kid, to the beach. It was great," the man says.

"Yeah. The beach is great. What do y'all do here?" Noah asks.

"I'm a chemist. Part of my job is to perform research on smell-related issues. The Fashion Institute of Technology was the birthplace for The Fragrance Foundation in 1949. A few years ago, in 1982, the Board of the Fragrance Foundation recognized a need for more research, so they established the Sense of Smell Institute. We were originally called the Olfactory Research Fund but changed the name. The Institute supports scientific and psychological research around the world in hospitals and universities. Our mission is to unravel the mysteries and the importance of the sense of smell. We also delve into the psychological benefits of fragrance."

"Would that be like aromatherapy?" Dane asks.

The man's smile is enormous, revealing a mouthful of large, brilliantly white teeth. "That is exactly right! What can we help you with?"

"Perfume sabotage. We've had deaths in Florida from ecstasy-laced perfumes."

"Oh, dear. We call that 'a fly in the juice.' It's becoming a serious problem, and we're looking for a way to combat it," the chemist says.

"A fly in the juice. Funny," Noah says.

"In the perfume industry, the liquid inside the bottle is called 'juice.' A 'fly' is an unintended substance that mars the product. You know, of course, that ecstasy has no odor. If it did, a 'nose' could detect it."

"We know what a nose is. My brother could be one," Noah says.

"Not now, I couldn't. My nose doesn't work right at

all. I can't identify anything that I'm smelling," Dane says.

"Sounds like you have Type I Hyposmia. It's an impairment of smell in which scents can still be detected but not recognized," the chemist says.

"Is it serious or permanent?" Dane asks.

"Not really. It originates in your olfactory epithelia area—it's the layer of roughly 15 million sensory cells that are in the upper-rear portion of your nose. It goes away on its own—like hay fever," the man says.

Dane exhales and rolls his eyes. "All I can smell is the city. How do you stand it?"

The chemist laughs. "Pretty rank, isn't it? You know how a coroner copes with autopsies on dead people? I do that, too. My jar of Vicks Vapor Rub® is my best friend some days. I'm sure your nose will be back to normal once you get back to Florida."

"Back to the problem at hand," Noah says. "How can we find this guy who is dosing the perfumes?"

"Well, ecstasy is a little like human pheromones. Undetectable to the nose but experienced on a much deeper olfactory level. They have pretty much the same effect on the wearer and the smeller. Generate that animal lust. We've found a way to isolate the presence of pheromones with a color-changing additive. We're hoping that same additive will alert manufacturers and sellers to the presence of other added substances."

"How's that work?"

"Pretty simple, actually. We are urging perfumers to add a small quantity of the colorless, odorless liquid to their juice. If the fragrance is tampered with, the juice turns black. Believe me. Nobody wants black perfume." The chemist smiles broadly, pleased with his explanation.

"Sounds like a great plan for the future, but our problem is the stuff on the street right now. The only lead we have is that the guy selling it has cancer. If he touches the bottle with his bare hands, my brother smells rotten oranges."

The chemist drops his clipboard and stares at the two men. "Your brother can smell cancer?" He looks around at the other technicians in the room, but they are busy at their work.

"If you can smell cancer...wow. Are you interested in staying a little while longer? I'd love to do some tests on your olfactory epithelia."

"Maybe another time. We've really got to get back. My fiancé is sick, and I can't smell anything right now anyway," Dane says as he inches toward the door.

"Will you leave your contact information? I really would like to talk with you more."

"Sure thing. I'll call you, O.K.? C'mon Noah. Gotta go," Dane says.

The chemist has a predatory look in his eye that is frightening. Dane exits the room with Noah in tow. He looks right and left, but the maze of hallways has him confused.

"Noah. I'm lost here," he gasps.

"Follow me," Noah says.

Noah runs down the hallways with Dane on his heels. "Stupid, stupid, stupid. I'm sorry, Dane. I'll keep my mouth shut from now on."

"Just don't tell people I can smell cancer. I don't want to be locked up like a lab rat in this stinking city."

Out on the street, the Lightfoot brothers once again join the crush of the citizens. The weather has taken a turn for the worse, and their coats are hardly suitable for the drizzling rain. Shivering, they keep as close to the buildings as the crowd allows. The sun has set, and the lights of the city blaze. To Noah's sensitive eyes, the lights are like a psychedelic acid trip. He clutches at Dane's sleeve to keep from veering off the sidewalk. Noah suddenly turns down a darkened alley for a respite.

"What a pair we are, bro. I can't smell, and you can't see. What good are psychic gifts if you can't use them, huh?" Dane says.

"I'm gonna be sick, Dane. I swear I am." Noah moans, and then he vomits.

Dane puts his arm around his brother protectively, trying to soothe him. "Almost there, Noah. Just a few more blocks, I think,"

A noise back in the alley attracts Dane's attention. A shape emerges. A tall man dressed in a navy-blue pea coat and a ski cap bounces forward, followed by a huskier man in grey sweats and a red hoodie. They eye the brothers while looking side to side, checking for any others in the alley. *Muggers,* Dane realizes.

"Well, lookie here. Two pretty boys having a sweet moment," the pea coat punk says making kissing sounds with his dry, chapped lips.

The hoodie mugger rushes up and grabs Noah's arms, pulling them behind his back painfully. "I've got this one," he says.

Pea coat shakes his hand out, and a knife appears. "I'm gonna get me a new hairdo," he says advancing on Dane.

Dane hunkers down in a battle stance, but he carries no weapon to use against a knife. His only chance is to circle around and keep clear of the blade. The man continues the kissing sounds and laughs, taunting his prey.

Noah struggles with the larger man, but he is weak from the nausea. The man slings him around, slamming his head against the brick wall. Noah crumples as all the lights go out.

"Noah!" Dane shouts, seeing his brother lying unconscious on the street.

The big man rushes Dane from behind, knocking him off his feet. Two well-aimed punches in the solar plexus leave him gasping for air. Suddenly, he feels his head jerked back as the man grabs his hair, pulling it tight and forcing him to look up at the mugger with the knife. Dane kicks out, but the man straddles his chest, immobilizing him. Reaching forward, the pea coat thug hacks through the hair held in his partner's hand. He jumps up holding a long black ponytail and waving it in the air.

"Whoop, whoop, whoop. I scalped me an Indian," the pea coat assailant cries.

Hoodie punches Dane in the jaw and gets to his feet, moving toward Noah. "I'm gonna scalp the other one," he says.

Just then, the alley is bathed in bright light, and a blaring horn sounds. The muggers' startled faces are illuminated as they back away from the light. A tall, lithe man jumps from the car and runs toward the two men. He carries a baseball bat in his right hand. The attackers run, but the man is faster. He swings the bat once, and hoodie falls to the ground. Another swing sends pea coat into the wall. He hits them both again, for good measure, before turning back.

Dane's vision is bleary, but he can see that the man is now coming toward Noah. The man reaches Noah and kneels beside him.

"Leave my brother alone," Dane huffs weakly.

The man puts his arm beneath Noah's arm and helps him into a standing position. Shuffling over to Dane, Noah drops down and embraces his brother.

"You alright? Oh jeez, Dane. They cut off your hair," Noah moans.

"Hair grows back, but if you dead, you dead," the

rescuer assures him.

"Thanks, mister. It's a good thing you came by."

"What you mean came by? Been following you all day. Why didn't you call Jaffey? Got in trouble, just like Jaffey said," the cabbie says.

"Jaffey? Oh, Jaffey. Thank you so much," Noah says.

"Tat's right. You are welcome. Now come, get in te car. Jaffey takin' you back to your hotel, and ten you gettin' outta tis city. New York is not for good Seminole boys like you." Jaffey walks them toward the car parked at the entrance to the alley.

Dane and Noah load up in the cab, and Jaffey drives them back to the hotel. He waits for them while they gather their yet unpacked bags and check out, and then he drives them straight to the airport. After getting their return tickets, he waits with them in the terminal until their flight is called.

There is not much talk. Each of them seems lost in their own thoughts. Noah nurses a bloody split in the side of his head, and Dane mourns the loss of his hair. Jaffey keeps his eyes on them like a strict chaperone. As they prepare to board, Dane reaches out and clasps Jaffey's hand.

"God bless you, brother. You saved our lives," Dane says, smiling weakly.

"Tank you for te blessing. Jaffey would save your life again, if he had to," Jaffey says.

The tall cabby opens Dane's hand and places a hank of long black hair in it. "Tat's all Jaffey could find. Sorry."

Dane regards the hair for a moment, and then hands it back to the man. "Keep it to remember me by. Hair grows back, like you said."

Without a thought, Jaffey pulls out a small pocket knife and slices off one long dreadlock. He holds it out to Dane. "Ten you keep tis to remember Jaffey by."

Dane takes the snakelike hair and clutches it in his fist, nodding, too moved for words.

"I don't have anything to give you, Jaffey, but I'll never be able to thank you enough," Noah says. "Dane says you were great with that baseball bat."

"You gave Jaffey a new name—C-v-f-e. Maybe Jaffey is a trickster rabbit after all, eh?" He gives Noah a slap-on-the-back hug.

The Lightfoot brothers bid Jaffey a bittersweet farewell and board their plane, happy to leave the Big Apple.

CHAPTER TWELVE
AWAKENING

HOURS LATER, DANE AND NOAH LIGHTFOOT disembark their airplane and enter the terminal. They are surprised to see Lee Thistleseed waiting for them. Dane looks at him quizzically, and Lee raises his bushy eyebrows in response. He walks forward and takes their carry-on bags.

"Kenny told me to come pick you up," Lee says. "He did not tell me about the haircut."

"Really?" Dane says, nodding, self-consciously running his fingers through his hacked-up tresses.

"Say what? Kenny told you? No way!" Noah says.

"Yes. It seems that my son may be awakening early," Lee confirms. Seventh children's powers usually begin manifesting around puberty. Lee's young son, Chenaniah is just barely past his twelfth birthday, so the presence of a psychic gift this soon comes as somewhat of a surprise to his father.

"What's his gift? Do you know yet?" Noah asks.

"It appears that Kenny experiences telepathic mind to mind communication," Lee says.

"What makes you think so?" Dane asks.

"Kenny woke me up to tell me that you two were flying home tonight. When I asked him how he knew, he said that a girl with a funny accent told him to 'send your father to the large bird building to get the brothers.' I took that to mean the airport. I have only been waiting for half an hour, and here you are," Lee says.

"That sounds like Kenny is channeling—like a medium. Who's this girl with the funny accent? Is she from the spirit world?" Dane asks.

"I have no idea. Kenny says she is not dead, but she lives far away. She can see him, and she talks to him in his head, but he does not see her" Lee says. "Tonight is the first time he has ever heard from her."

"Is that all she said? 'Send your father to the large bird building for the brothers.' That's kindof odd—like she doesn't know what an airport is," Dane says.

"That is all she said. I got up quietly, left a note, and did not wake Wren. I sent Kenny back to bed. I suppose I will have to deal with this in the morning," Lee says.

"A telepath in the family. Now that's exciting," Noah says.

"Exciting? If you say so. If my son is channeling a telepath, then he is the first one I have ever encountered. I am woefully unprepared to train him," Lee says with a frown.

"Life is full of challenges, huh?" Noah says, clapping his mentor on the back.

Distracted by the emergence of Kenny's clairvoyant gift, the Lightfoot men forget their harrowing New York alley experience for the time being and chat amiably while they pile into Lee's car; however, during the ride from the Tallahassee airport to Lee's home, they grow quiet. Dane finds himself reaching for hair that is no longer there, and Noah gently palpates the bruised split on the side of his face. They are both lost in their thoughts, and Lee knows better than to interrupt them. There will be plenty of time when they get back to his house.

Lee pulls into his carport, and the three men silently climb the back steps to the breakfast room. As they enter the house, they are greeted by the sight of Wren, Shine, and Kenny sitting in their pajamas at the picnic-style breakfast table. Shine has an array of antiseptics, cotton balls, butterfly bandages, and antibacterial ointments on the table in front of her. Wren clutches a pair of scissors, a large towel, and a bottle of baby powder. Kenny sits on the bench at the head of the table with his back to the bow window, sipping a cup of hot chocolate piled high with floating marshmallows.

"What is all this?" Lee asks his wife.

Wren shrugs and nods in her son's direction. "After you left to pick up the boys, Kenny told us to gather these things and wait for y'all. I guess he already knew that we'd need them."

Everyone looks at the boy who is innocently drinking from the mug. Young Chenaniah Thistleseed is named for the Biblical Chief of the Levites whose name meant "established by God." Chenaniah, a highly skilled and honorable man, was hand-picked by King David and the elders of Israel to lead the musicians and oversee those who carried the Ark of the Covenant of the Lord from the house of Obed-edom to Jerusalem. Nicknamed Kenny by the other children, the young namesake gives them all a radiant smile, complete with a milk chocolate mustache.

"Yep. The girl told me we needed a 'healer and a shearer' for when you get here. I didn't know what a 'shearer' was, so I asked Shine. She said it was somebody who cuts hair. I figured Mom could do that real good," he says. "Did I do alright?"

"You did great, buddy," Noah says. "A fourth-year vet tech and a mother with sewing scissors work out just fine."

"Well, I guess you two better take a seat and let us women fix you up," Shine says.

Noah straddles the bench Shine offers, and she goes to work cleaning and disinfecting his wound. The split is not deep, but it is long—running in a curved line from his right temple to just in front of his ear. Shine takes great care as she works, and Noah is thankful for her gentle touch. She is truly turning into a great veterinarian with her compassionate spirit and confident manner. Her fingers prod and push the skin together, meeting the edges of the cut smoothly, and then taping them with the butterfly bandages so there is no puckering. When she finishes, she leans back and scrutinizes her work.

"So, tell me. What's the prognosis, 'Doctor' Shine Thistleseed?" Noah asks.

"Not a doctor yet but working on it. Won't be much longer. As for your cut—it should heal well with just a tiny scar line. I'll keep checking it to make sure. You keep your hands off your face, and don't pick at it, and it'll be alright. I can't do anything for the ugly, though. You'll just have to live with that face for the rest of your life" she says.

"Ha ha. Thanks, Shine," Noah says. "Hey, Kenny. How about some hot cocoa for the wounded? Plenty of marshmallows for me."

Kenny is happy to oblige. He hops up from his perch and goes to the stove to pour a mug for his friends. In the meantime, Wren does her best to give Dane a haircut that will hide the butchering he received. There is no way to salvage any of the length because of the way the mugger hacked it off at the crown of his head. Her only choice is to clip it close enough all over to make it match.

Dane keeps his eyes closed, not looking at the black locks piling up around his feet. When Wren finishes, she dusts off his neck with talcum powder, and Shine hurriedly sweeps up the cuttings into a dustpan.

"Wow, Dane! You are looking so GQ now." Kenny whistles his approval.

"GQ?" his mother says. "What do you mean by that, Kenny?"

"*Gentlemen's Quarterly Magazine*," Shine says. "It's a magazine featuring fashionably elegant men and women."

"Oh, I see," Wren says. "And how do you know about that, young man?"

Kenny looks embarrassed. "The twins showed me. They said it had 'cute guys' in it. I didn't notice much about the guys, except they all had those short haircuts like Dane's. I looked at *all* the pretty girls, though." Kenny grins and rolls his eyes.

"Kenny's awakening," Noah smirks.

"Oh, no he's not," Wren says. "Kenny's going to bed. Now, child."

She flicks the towel at his bottom, and the boy runs laughing up the stairs.

While Shine and Wren tidy up the kitchen, the men move into the adjacent family room, each taking his favorite seat. Lee chooses the large wing back chair with its well-worn footstool. Dane piles up on the loveseat, and Noah takes his usual place on the plush rug in front of the fireplace, a balled-up afghan beneath his head.

"Perhaps you feel like talking now," Lee says.

"That was not my favorite trip," Noah says. "Who knew so many things could happen in just one day? I don't even know where to start."

"Let's begin with the most recent events. What happened to your face and your brother's hair?"

Dane and Noah look at each other, and the older brother gets the nod.

"We got mugged," Dane says. "We slipped into an alley to escape the sights and smells of the city..."

"...I got sick and puked. I've never seen so many lights and colors and people and cars. I thought my eyes were going to pop out..." Noah says.

"...and what a stench! I thought I'd never breathe fresh air again."

"Then these characters came out of nowhere. My head was down—because I was barfing, you know—and one of them pinned my arms behind me. The next thing I knew, my head exploded. I don't remember what happened after that."

"The one mugger slammed Noah into the wall. I saw him go down, and I thought he was dead. The other one had a knife, so I was watching him at the same time..."

"...we had to stash our knives in our luggage to get on the plane."

"So anyway, the big guy caught me and wrestled me to the ground. He grabbed my hair, and the other one chopped it off." Dane runs his fingers through his scalp. "Then they said they were gonna scalp Noah."

During the men's tag-team explanation, Wren and

Shine move into the room and take their places at each end of the couch. They look from one brother to the other as the story unfolds.

"All of a sudden, this car screeches into the alley, and the driver jumps out swinging a baseball bat. He hits both the muggers and knocks them out, and then he goes over to Noah. I'm thinking he's another mugger, so I come after him, but it turns out that he's our Jamaican cab driver from earlier in the day," Dane says.

"And get this. His name is 'Jah-FEE.' He spelled it different but pronounced it the same as our Creek word for…" Noah says.

"Trickster Rabbit," both brothers say in unison.

"Jaffey had been following us all day because he figured we'd get into trouble. I guess he was like our guardian angel, because if he hadn't come along, I think those punks might have killed us," Dane says.

"Yeah. He took us right then to the airport and made sure we left New York," Noah says. "Oh! And I almost forgot! He gave Dane one of his hairy dreadlocks to remember him by."

During the story, Shine's mouth drops lower and lower. But she's not the only one. Her parents have the same expression. Even the cool-and-calm Lee Thistleseed finds himself speechless and gawking…and afraid. Once again, he has almost lost his adopted sons. A rumbling sound draws his attention. Noah's stomach. Wren also hears the noise.

"Boys, it's late and I know you must be hungry after such an adventure. I've got plenty of leftover vegetable soup and cornbread," she says, pulling Shine up to help her in the kitchen.

With the women out of the room for a while, Lee shifts the conversation to the subject of the tainted perfumes and the reason the men went to New York in the first place.

"What did you boys find out about the ecstasy?" Lee says.

"Evidently, ecstasy is a real problem in New York, but they haven't had any incidences of ecstasy-laced perfumes," Dane says.

Noah sits up and leans his back against the hearth. "They knew about 'The Mister' at the police station—nice people, by the way—but they haven't been able to locate him. They said that he was part of a huge counterfeit fragrance ring, but he's working alone now, peddling his product down here."

"We don't have a name or a face for this 'Mister' character, but we know that his stuff made its way to the boutique in town where I bought Raven's perfume.

Suddenly, Dane sits straight up, and his hands immediately go to his head. "Raven! Oh, no. What am I going to tell her?" He jumps up off the couch and begins heading out of the family room.

"And where do you think you're going?" Wren says, stopping him at the doorway.

"I need to go to the hospital," Dane says.

"No, you don't. Raven is fine. She's back at her apartment, and she has…"

"…she has an in-home nurse tending her around the clock. Sit back down and eat some soup and cornbread. You boys are staying here tonight," Lee says.

"That's right," Shine says, placing a tray on the enormous slice of a cypress stump that serves as the coffee table. "Shelly's sleeping on a pallet in Selah's room, and I'm in Shell's room. Debby and Zorah are having a sleepover out back in my cottage, so you guys get the twin beds upstairs in their room. See! All the sleeping arrangements have been made, thanks to Kenny's heads- up."

Noah slides up to the coffee table and grabs a square of cornbread. "No objections on my end," he says, crumbling it into a huge cup of soup.

Dane sits back down on the couch and resigns himself to letting the Thistleseed women fret over him. The vegetable soup is a welcome balm after a day of unintentional fasting. He leans over the mug and inhales the steam, relieved to note that, although faint, he can detect ham, onion, celery, tomatoes, carrots, basil, oregano, green peppers. *Ahhhh, it smells like home again.*

CHAPTER THIRTEEN
ON THE SCENT TRAIL

THE NEXT MORNING, DANE AND NOAH awake to the intoxicating smell of hickory smoked bacon frying.

"Mmmmm. Smell that? Man's favorite scent," Noah says, bolting from the bed and disappearing into the bathroom. Seconds later, he splashes water on his face and hands and sprints through the bedroom door. His footfalls pound as he descends the stairs two at a time.

Rising from the other bed, Dane ambles to the sink and washes his face. Reaching for the towel, he is shocked at his appearance in the six-foot wide vanity mirror. He has forgotten about his hair. He studies himself in the mirror for a while and wonders irrationally if Raven will still love him without his long, silky mane. Anxious to see her, he quickly finishes his ablations and wanders down the stairs to the dining room.

Wren has prepared a breakfast of mammoth

proportions, but in a household of ten, the addition of two more people doesn't require much change in cooking style. So that everyone can enjoy the visit of the Lightfoot brothers, the youngest children have been given honorary folding chairs at the corners of the table. Nobody minds the extra crowding.

After a sweet blessing on the food by little Shelly, the serving bowls are passed clockwise. The older boys dub this process "he who hesitates is hungry." Needless to say, the bowls pass quickly. At the end of the serving frenzy, Dane's plate is layered with fluffy scrambled eggs, creamy cheese grits, crispy bacon, and fat buttermilk biscuits covered in heavily peppered white sausage gravy.

The dining room is not a place for discussing business; it is a time for family to share their week. This Saturday morning is no different. Shelly is proud of the "A" on her spelling test, Kenny is finally catching on to long division, Debby and Zorah are struggling with driver's education, Selah is sitting by a cute guy in her chemistry class at the junior college, Bill thinks he may change his major to engineering, Cy is working extra hours at his job to save up for his own apartment, and Shine gets to neuter a dog all by herself at work next week.

Long after the serving bowls and plates are scraped, sopped, and some are even licked clean, the family remains at the table, reluctant to leave the company of those they love.

Lee pushes his chair back and stands, and that

signals the end of the meal. Wren and the children clear the table and begin the breakfast clean up. Everyone has his or her own chore, and they work like a well-oiled machine.

Lee, Dane, and Noah resume their favorite places in the family room to map out a plan of action. Even though their trip ended suddenly, much was learned in the men's misadventure.

"My first stop is Raven's, if you don't mind. I want to check on her, and she needs to see my new look," Dane says, running his hand across his head.

"It's actually a pretty good haircut, all things considered. Too bad it shows more of your face, though," Noah says.

"It is only hair, Dane. Hair grows back," Lee says.

"Hey, that's what Jaffey said, too," Noah says laughing.

"A wise man, your taxi driver," Lee says. "Alright, then. Dane, after you visit Raven, I would like for you to go to the boutique where you purchased her perfume. Ask questions about vendors, employees, purchasers, anyone who may have had contact with 'The Mister.' Try to sniff out more of the tainted fragrances. If you encounter any, do not touch them. Call Jack. He can confiscate the items before they are sold to any other hapless customers."

Dane nods in agreement. Lee turns to Noah. "You and I are going tracking. It is imperative that we locate this man. We need to know where he is today and alert the police in that area—maybe even make a physical trip to the location," he says.

Noah pales. "I—uh—I really would prefer not to go back to New York, if you don't mind."

Lee smiles. "Of course not. If he is in New York, I will take Graham."

Noah exhales in relief, and then he lifts his head and looks quizzically at the foyer door.

"Ken, my man. What's up?" Noah says.

Heads turn as Kenny enters the room frowning. He walks up to his father.

"Dad?" Kenny says. "She says to look south."

"The man is in the south, son?" Lee asks.

"Yes...with a lady. He's dying."

Lee gives his son a crooked, somewhat sad, smile and gently pats his cheek. "Thank you, son. And thank your friend."

"I already did," Kenny says, walking out of the room.

The three men shake their head, speechless. Finally, Lee breaks the silence.

"Get your bags, boys. We must move quickly. I will call Graham and have him meet us at your house, Noah. Dane, I will drop you at your place, and then you can drive to Raven's."

Dane and Noah race up the stairs while Lee steps into the kitchen to fetch his wife. Wren meets him at the door, drying her hands with a dishtowel, and gives him a quick kiss on the mouth. Lee waves to the rest of the kids and climbs in his vehicle, the Lightfoots on his heels. Ten seconds later, they are on the road.

* * *

Ten minutes later, they arrive at Dane's house. Without even bothering to go inside and change clothes, Dane jumps into his car and heads off toward Raven's apartment. His heart pounds like a teenager on his first date all the way there.

Walking up to her door, he summons up his resolve and knocks, pasting a smile on his face. He can smell the sage smoldering from inside, and his smile becomes more relaxed. *She's using my mother's gifts, I bet.* The smile becomes an "O" when the door opens, and he is face to face…with Fawn.

"Mom? What are you doing here?"

"Why, I'm taking care of my future daughter-in-law. I told you she was sick."

"Yes, you told me so. But who told you? How did you know?" he questions as he enters.

She closes the door and locks it. "Wren Thistleseed is my friend, son. She called me as soon as Lee left for the hospital. I took the bus and got here just in time to take Raven home when she was released. Come, now. You can't have all the fun."

Dane takes his mother in his arms and holds her tightly. "I love you, Mom. You have always, always been there for me."

"And I always, always will." Pulling back, she just now notices his hair. Her eyes widen as she studies his face, but she keeps quiet, knowing he will explain in his own time.

Dane kisses Fawn on the cheek and shrugs, then walks down the hall to Raven's bedroom. He pushes the door open slightly and sees her lying on the bed, propped up against several pillows and covered with a soft patchwork quilt that must have come from Fawn. Raven's eyes are closed, and she is napping.

He scans the room and sees evidence of Fawn's healing remedies everywhere—sage smoking in a large clamshell on the dresser, an intricately woven dream catcher with downy feathers hanging above the head of the bed, a sun-bleached turtle shell bowl filled with fragrant herbs on one nightstand, and an empty cup of what is surely Fawn's blessed healing tea on the other. *Yep. Mom's taking good care of her.*

His gaze goes back to the dresser, and he spots a dozen or more crystal perfume bottles of different shapes and sizes—all labeled *DeVanille*. One is like a round bull's eye target with a red circular label in its center, another is square with a stopper resembling a crown, and one very large bottle is shaped as a deep bowl on a stand with a royal blue semicircular stopper. A smaller bottle is shaped similarly, but with a more fluted bowl and stand. Tucked here and there are others that are taller, more elongated, ribbed, topped with gold caps, mushroom shaped stoppers, triangular crystal stoppers, and, of course, the gold filigreed atomizer that was her engagement present.

Looking at the bottles, Dane feels the hair on his arms raise. *This is what made her sick.* He quietly walks to the dresser and sniffs deeply in each bottle, trying to detect the rotten orange smell of "The Mister's" cancerous touch.

"Colored water," Raven whispers.

Startled, Dane whirls around to face his fiancé. Even pale and sick in bed, she is breathtakingly beautiful. He rushes to her side and falls on his knees, gently stroking her lovely face with his hands. She smiles, and his heart thumps in his chest. Her hand stretches out and her fingers sift through his short hair. He turns his head and kisses her palm, tears squeezing out from the corners of his eyes.

"Babe, I'm so sorry," he exhales. "I should've known something was wrong."

Dane looks in Raven's eyes and sees only love there—no blame, no judgment. She reaches up and pulls his head to her chest, her fingers entwined in his short locks. They stay locked in that position for a long time. Then Dane sits back on his haunches.

"What did you say to me a while ago?"

"Colored water. Your mother dumped out all the perfumes and washed the bottles. She filled them with colored water and fragrant herbs. And *Voila*. All-natural perfumes—no unnatural additives. And each one has a different scent. My own personal array of aromatherapies. Go ahead. Sniff them out. I think all the poison is gone."

"If my mother did it, I know it's all gone. She'd make sure of that."

"That's right. You better not doubt me, boy," Fawn says entering the room. She carries a steaming cup of tea to Raven and also hands one to Dane.

"I'm not sick, Mom," he protests.

"Maybe not, but I see a bruise under your eye, and I don't think you cut your hair on purpose!" She sits on the edge of the bed and looks at him. "We're waiting."

Having no choice but to give his story to the two insistent women, Dane tells them everything—from the sensory overload of the city, to the Fashion Institute of Technology, to the Sense of Smell Institute, to the mugging in the alley. When he finishes, they just stare at him.

Finally, Raven breaks the tension. "Well, I'm disappointed. I wanted you to bring me something from Macy's!"

Laughing, Fawn ruffles Dane's hair and quickly disappears into the kitchen. Moments later, she comes out bringing a tray loaded with mugs of chicken soup, soda crackers, and cheddar cheese cubes for the three of them. They sit around Raven's bedroom eating and chattering like nothing has ever happened. After lunch, Dane explains that he is going to the boutique to search for clues about the perfume saboteur.

"You sleep, Babe. I'll be back pretty soon. I'm not wearing my crime fighting uniform today. I'm only investigating," he says, kissing her forehead.

"If you promise to be careful."

"I will. Sweet dreams."

"No problem with that," Fawn says. "That's a very special dream catcher over her bed."

Dane moves closer to inspect it. Taking a look at the feathers, he laughs. "Emma. Give her my thanks."

"Emma was happy to oblige. She has plenty more feathers." Fawn walks her son to the door and gives him a hug. Slipping her hand into his back pocket, she pulls out a folded flyer. "What's this?"

"Oh, just some literature this animal activist gave us in New York. You can have it. But what are you doing in my pocket, anyway?"

"Emma sent you a protection totem."

He reaches back and pulls out the totem—a sprig of sage and a long grey goose feather, wrapped together with embroidery floss. He clutches it and embraces his mother.

"I swear, Mom. You and that goose have a peculiar relationship," he says as he leaves.

"That we do," Fawn says walking into the bedroom. "What can I get you, Raven?"

Raven smiles warmly at her future mother-in-law. "One more cup of tea would be super, and then I'm going to take a nap."

Fawn sets the flyer down on the night stand and picks up the lunch tray. Curious, Raven reaches over and takes the folded paper. She casually reads the back, then opens to the middle and scans the article. It details the endangerment of the African civet—a cat-like animal in the mongoose family used by perfume manufacturers for a base note fixative.

According to the pamphlet, The World Society for the Protection of Animals states that the animal's anal glands produce a musky substance. Sometimes, the animals are killed, and the glands are removed. More often, the animals are kept in tiny cages, and their musk is harvested every few days by scraping the substance out of the anal sacs by means of a special tiny silver spoon, a procedure that is painful and inhumane. *Sounds barbaric,* Raven thinks.

Turning the pamphlet to the front, Raven freezes. There, on the front cover, is a picture of an African civet—identical to the cat with both stripes and spots and the long muzzle she drew while tracking on the way home from Tampa, complete with the tiny spoon. Raven screams, and Fawn comes running.

* * *

Dane's tires screech as he slams on the brakes just in time to keep from rear ending the car in front of him. Pulling his attention back to the road, he locates Connie's Cottage—a quaint boutique housed in a wood-frame building on the banks of Lake Jackson. Its clientele includes up-scale men and women who desire trendy, runway inspired clothing and the fashion industry's latest designs. The atmosphere is hoity-toity, and the wares are expensive, making it *"the"* place to be seen shopping. Dane was referred by another deputy fire marshal, not because the man shops there, but because a friend of a friend of his wife does.

Inside the store, Dane walks slowly up and down the aisles, trying to pick up the scent of the bottles that have the odor of moldy oranges...and there are several, although the smell is very faint. He is aware of the impeccably made-up saleswoman who begins to follow him. He turns to her.

"Excuse me, ma'am, but I need some help with your fragrances," he says.

The woman smiles broadly, revealing perfectly uniform, braces-straightened teeth behind her glossy red lips. "Of course," she says. "My name is Helene. Are you looking for a gift?"

"Well, not exactly. I came in here a couple of weeks ago and bought a small dispenser of *DeVanille*. I need to know where you got it."

The woman's smile twitches slightly and she appears puzzled. "We have suppliers that provide us with our fragrance products. Were you wanting to purchase some more?"

"No, I need to know who you purchased it from."

"I'm sorry, but it could have been one of many vendors. I'll be glad to order it for you." Her hand flutters up to the clunky gold necklace around her throat.

"No. I just need to know your source. Was it a company or an individual?"

"I don't know. Why are you asking me? Janie Hiller did our ordering, but she moved away a few days ago. She has a sick family member down south that she was going to care for. Do you want to buy something or not?"

"Ma'am—Helene. I don't want to alarm you, but quite a few of your perfumes have been tampered with. If you don't mind, I'm going to use your phone and call for some help from the police," he says. Seeing her frightened look, he adds, "You aren't in trouble. But I need you to find out where Janie moved. It's very important. We don't want anyone else to die."

"Die? People have died from our perfume? Oh my gosh," she squeaks.

Dane moves to the phone. "Just get Janie's personnel file and anything else that may help us find her. If you need to phone a supervisor, you can do that after I'm done. And don't touch any of the perfume bottles. They're dangerous."

The saleswoman wrings her hands and nods while Dane calls Jack Abernathy. By the time he finishes the call, she has found a forwarding address for Janie Hiller...in a Tampa suburb.

* * *

Noah, Lee, and Graham sit at the small oak pedestal table in Noah's kitchen deciphering the track from which

Lee has just returned. So far, they identify a wooded area in the outskirts of Tampa, with felled branches all around a brown and white cinder block house. Outside the house is the "steed as black as night, a fearsome cat poised to run"—the black jaguar belonging to "The Mister." According to Lee, the "cat is cold, and brown leaves sleep on its head," indicating that the car has not been driven recently, perhaps in the last day or two. This is consistent with the fact that Noah and Dane could not locate the man in New York.

Noah's track of the man reveals a numerical address and a street sign, as well as a glimpse of the man lying on a bed in a darkened room with grayish skin and dark circles ringing his eyes. It is apparent to all of them that "The Mister" is gravely ill from the cancer. Noah also sees several cardboard boxes in the room filled with perfume bottles.

Graham's track gives them more insight about the severity of the man's illness. His voice is raspy and weak, punctuated by frequent deep chest coughing. As to any other occupants of the house, he hears a woman who tends to the man. From their conversation, they are not lovers, but they do seem to be related.

"I bet they're brother and sister," Noah says.

"And I'd take that bet," Graham concurs.

"Alright, gentlemen. Let us see what we have. 'The Mister' is on his death bed, being cared for by his sister. They are in a brown block house with white trim at 6475 Lovie Lane in a suburb of Tampa. The woman has a lot of pets, according to Graham," Lee says.

"Yeah. Thanks for the zoo impressions, Gray. Really entertaining," Noah laughs.

"The presence of the animals indicates that the house is more remote than just being out of the city limits. All the tree limbs lead me to reason that this was an area damaged by Hurricane Andrew," Lee says.

"Downtown Tampa escaped the worst of the storm, but the outlying areas seem to have been hit pretty hard," Noah says.

A car door slamming outside draws their attention to the living room, and in walks Dane.

They quickly bring him up to speed about what they each learned in their tracks, and he gives them the name of the woman, Janie Hiller. The excitement is electric. These are men who love solving puzzles and saving lives. If they had superpowers instead of psychic powers, they would be akin to the Justice League of America. But they are ordinary human beings, subject to mental and physical ills and the fragility of mortality. Nonetheless, they are ersatz super heroes—brave and selfless and determined.

"So, who goes?" Noah asks.

"I'm going," Dane replies.

"Not without me," Noah says.

"Here we go again," Graham moans.

"Boys, I think it will be better if I go alone, this time," Lee says, giving them each a solemn nod.

"No way," Dane argues.

"Dane. You and Noah have just gone through a nerve wracking experience. I can bring a fresh perspective to this situation, as well as pinpoint the location," Lee explains.

"But Raven..." Dane says.

"Raven needs you here," Lee states. "I can't risk something happening to you."

"She doesn't need me as long as my mom's with her. I'm going to Tampa," he insists.

"Hey, ya'll. I'm bigger and a better fighter. If there's trouble, I need to be there to help Lee," Graham says holding up his beefy fists.

"Graham makes a good point," Lee says.

The four of them get louder and louder as they each jockey for position. Through all the noise, they don't even realize that the front door has opened until it slams closed. They instantly stop talking and crowd into the living room, surprised to see Shine standing there.

"Sorry, guys, but there's a change in plans. Dad, you and Graham need to load up in the SUV. It's gassed up and ready to go to Tampa. Dane, go to Raven's and stay with her. You, too, Noah. Your mother's waiting for you," she says.

"Hey! Who died and made you the Queen of the castle, Shine?" Noah says.

"Nobody's dead yet, and that's how it's gonna stay," she bristles, eyebrows raised, ready for a challenge.

"Shinehah. I appreciate you preparing the vehicle.

Dane can drive you home," Lee says.

"No, Dad. I'm not going home. I'm going with you and Graham," she states.

"Says who?" Graham objects. "It's too dangerous for you. I won't allow it."

All heads turn to Graham. "You won't allow it?" Noah says grinning.

"Oh, step off, Noah," Graham says, causing a burst of laughter from the brothers.

"Shinehah. This is not a matter for you, sweetheart," her father says.

"Kenny said I had to go. He even packed my vet-med kit with things he said I'd need," she says. "The girl said for the three of us to go now, before the man dies."

Graham looks confused. "Since when does Kenny tell us what to do?"

"Sorry, Gray. We should've already told you about him. Kenny's waking up, and he's channeling a telepath," Noah says.

Graham pokes out his lower lip, pulls his wire-rimmed glasses down on his nose, and nods. "That's cool. O.K. Let's do what Kenny says. Load up."

Graham and Shine head for the car, leaving the Lightfoot brothers with their hands in their pockets. Lee takes a deep breath. Then he walks over to the men and puts his arms around their shoulders, pulling them both in for a long hug.

"Stay together, boys. Do not separate. Do you understand me? I need you—all three of you—to stay together in case we need you to track," Lee says.

"Will do, Hona. You can contact us at Raven's apartment. Find this guy and do whatever you have to. And please, be careful," Dane says.

Lee smiles and releases the men. Walking through the open door, he turns back and waves. Dane and Noah both jerk their chins up in an identical gesture of good-bye. As the SUV drives away from the curb with Graham at the wheel, the Lightfoot brothers pull the front door shut and make their way to Noah's mustang to reunite with Raven and their mother.

CHAPTER FOURTEEN
<u>RAIN AND SHINE</u>

ONE HOUR AFTER TURNING ONTO I-4 the weather suddenly turns bad. The clouds make good on their threat of rain. Lee is glad that Graham is driving, and his oldest daughter is securely buckled into her seat belt in the back. The wind buffets the car, but Graham has an iron grip. To pass the time, Lee fills him in on the powers that Kenny suddenly displays. Quiet and thoughtful in contrast to the Lightfoot brothers, Graham listens carefully and takes it all in before he comments.

"Chenaniah is twelve, now. That is an important time in a boy's life. Were he of Jewish descent, he would be on the verge of manhood. And among my people, he would be ready for a spirit journey," Graham says.

"Among mine, as well; however, we are so-called modern Indians now. We have no rites of passage as in the early days of our people," Lee says.

Graham smiles without turning his eyes on his friend. "I suspect that your son's journey into second-sightedness is more closely geared to your rites of passage than his," Graham says.

"You are very intuitive, Graham. I feel this responsibility quite keenly. I am afraid of making a mistake in his training."

"Mistakes are always possible, Lee, but I seriously doubt you'll err in his training. Besides, you know I'll help you all I can."

Lee reaches over and places his leathery hand on Graham's broad right shoulder. The men seem to have an unspoken understanding, more sophisticated than the father-son relationship he holds with Dane and Noah. *How I would welcome Graham as my son-in-law*, Lee thinks.

The four-hour trip to the Tampa Bay area stretches to five because of the inclement weather. By the time they arrive at their exit, the rain is heavy, and visibility is limited. As the back-seat navigator, Shine scans the street signs for their landmarks.

"There," she says. "Turn right at that street just up ahead. Then we go down four stoplights and take a left."

Graham obediently follows her directions, being careful to avoid limbs on the street. Shine does a masterful job of navigating, and before long they arrive at Lovie Lane. The residential landscape has changed from condos to apartments to neighborhoods to a smattering of homes with large expanses of woods in between.

Lovie Lane is a hard-packed clay road unmaintained by the county. Graham gingerly picks his way between water filled potholes, thankful that Kenny's telepathic partner told him the weather would be bad, and Shine had the presence of mind to drive the rugged SUV.

Thinking of Shine makes his stomach flutter, so he pulls his mind back to negotiating the road. The absence of ruts tells him that nobody has left the house since before the rainstorm. He is relieved to see the small block house up ahead. Suddenly, a strong gust of wind rocks the vehicle, and Graham skids to a stop just as a large tree limb falls in front of them, blocking their way.

Having no choice but to go to the house on foot, Lee, Graham, and Shine exit the vehicle, clothed in the clear plastic slickers Kenny has packed in Shine's medical kit. They approach the front door, and Lee knocks heavily. The door opens, and a semi-attractive woman in her late forties blinks at them.

"Yes? Can I help you?" she says. Looking out the door, she sees the limb blocking the road in front of the car. She turns back at the group and surmises that they are lost travelers who have been stranded. "You're soaked. Please, come on in. You can use my phone."

Taking her lead, the three of them enter the house, taking in the simple hominess of the furnishings. Janie Hiller is a sweet woman, trying hard to do the right thing for a group of strangers. It's hard for them to believe that the brother she harbors is a drug dealer and a killer.

Shine pretends to call a tow service, all the while scanning the rooms around her. Sitting on a chair near the telephone, she feels a tail swipe against her foot. *A kitten*, she decides. Hanging up the phone, she wags her fingers near the floor and is rewarded with a tiny paw darting from under the chair.

"Here, kitty, kitty, kitty," she coos. A tiny animal peeks around the chair leg. Shine flattens her hand on the floor, and the kitten crawls into her open palm. She picks it up and holds it against her chest, scratching behind its rounded, tufted ears. It curls into a ball and rests comfortably in her arms.

In the kitchen, Lee and Graham sit at the modest table talking to their hostess. When Shine enters, Janie's eyes widen, and she stops talking. Shine takes a seat, holding the warm ball of fur on her lap.

"I love your kitten," Shine says. "I've never seen one with this coloring—almost like a raccoon with its mask and stripes, but it has spots, too. It's beautiful."

"Thank you. She's a very sweet little thing. A rescue animal," Janie says.

"She's quite an unusual looking kitten. Where did you get her?" Lee says.

Janie stands up nervously. "She was just wandering around outside."

"Really? She seems to be very young. I wonder where her littermates are," Lee presses. "Did you see a mother cat anywhere?"

"Why are you so interested in a stray cat?" Janie is wary, looking back and forth at the visitors.

Graham has also been studying the animal. Its muzzle is elongated more than normal, and there are other peculiarities about it that bring to mind a picture he has recently seen. He stares back at Janie.

"I'm sorry, Ms. Hiller, but this is no ordinary kitten, is it?"

"How do you know my name?" Alarmed, Janie Hiller backs away into the living room. Lee and Graham rise and follow her, but Shine stays seated at the table, holding tight to the tiny creature.

"I think you should go back to your car now. My brother is very sick, and I have to give him some medicine. Please. I really want you to leave," she pleads.

"We aren't threatening you, Ms. Hiller. We know about your brother, and we want to help you," Graham says.

"No. No. You'll take him to jail, and he'll die there. He's all I have. I'm taking good care of him. They were going to throw those testers away, so it's not really stealing. He's very ill. We need the money for medicine. Don't arrest him." She begins to cry.

"Ms. Hiller. We are not the police. Your brother has been putting a narcotic into those perfumes. People are sick from it. Some people have died. We just need to get the perfumes off the street so no other people are harmed," Lee says.

"No. Edgar wouldn't hurt anybody. He was putting human pheromones into the perfumes. You know—to make people more attractive—to make them fall in love, and then they'd want to buy more. They're harmless. I know. I did the research." Janie wrings her hands.

"No, ma'am. He put ecstasy into those fragrances. It's a drug that is dangerous," Graham explains. "Teenagers bought those testers and died."

"I don't believe you. They're pheromones. I would never agree to drugs. I love people. I love animals. I'm against the inhumane testing of products on animals, so why would I let him hurt people?"

"You have other animals here?"

"I—I have some others. They were lab animals—dogs, cats, a couple of beavers. They were being tortured so women could have tear-free mascara or use shampoo that wouldn't sting their eyes. Some of them—like the African civet pup that your girl is holding—are kept in cages for years just to get oils and glands that are used in perfumes."

"How did you come by these animals?" Lee asks.

"I went to New York with Edgar once, and he took me to a lab. When I saw those poor animals in the cages, I knew I had to rescue them. We rented a truck and freed them one night after the lab was closed. Edgar had a key. The mother civet had been so traumatized that she died before we got back to Florida, leaving this one pup an orphan. We did a *good* thing by saving them!"

"Ms. Hiller. Where is Edgar? He has cancer. He is dying. He does not have much time. Let us talk to him."

Janie Hiller looks uncertainly at a closed door, and then back at Graham and Lee. Tears streaming down her face, she points at the door.

"Please don't hurt him," she begs.

Lee takes her hand and looks kindly into her eyes. "We are not in the hurting business, dear lady. We are the good guys," he says, helping her to a well-worn club chair.

Graham starts to open the door but stops. "Ms. Hiller? Is your brother armed?"

Janie shakes her head, and Graham tentatively opens the door. Even though his psychic gift is clairaudience, he can smell the impending death coming from the man on the bed. Graham is relieved that Lee ordered Dane to stay home. The odor is wretched. He walks to the bed and looks down at the man.

"Edgar Hiller? My name is Graham Skysong, and I'm here to help you obtain a better place in the land of the spirits. Do you understand me?"

Hiller turns his head toward Graham. He blinks his eyes twice, which Graham takes to mean, "yes." Graham takes his hand. It is dry and papery—the hand of a desiccated corpse.

"Mr. Hiller. The drugs you put in the fragrances have killed people. Have you put any more perfumes out on the streets in the past week?"

Hiller shakes his head ever so slightly. He shifts his eyes to a stack of cardboard boxes against the wall. Lee enters the room and walks to the pile of boxes and opens the top. Inside are decorative boxes of high-end perfumes. He notes their names: *Romarin, Arômes, Céleste, Chatoyant No. 2, Épice d'Asie, Séduisant, DeVanille.* In the carton at the top of the next stack are smaller boxes—the testers Hiller hands out at the clubs.

"Is that all of them, Mr. Hiller?" Graham asks, to which he receives two blinks. Graham turns to Lee. "Lee, please bring Mr. Hiller's sister in. He's going soon."

Janie Hiller walks slowly over to the bed. Sitting on the edge, she takes her brother's hands in her own. Her tears wet his face. He looks up to her and struggles to speak. Unable to make sound, he mouths the words, "I love you." And then he exhales his last breath and is gone.

Janie lays her head on Edgar's chest and cries aloud. Quietly, in the background underneath the sound of her weeping, a song emanates from the big Navajo. He sings to guide the spirit to the sky. And silently, Lee adds a prayer.

* * *

Twenty minutes later, Lovie Lane is a hub of activity. Chief Lew Rowan, a squad car of officers, and a medical examiner arrive. The tree limb has been removed, and a couple of animal control trucks park near the house. The officers are busy loading the trucks with all manner of animals found behind Janie Hiller's house. Shine clutches tightly to the civet in her arms, watching the animals being rescued, reluctant to give up the tiny civet pup.

The body of Edgar Hiller is placed in a black body bag and removed for autopsy. Officers carefully load the cardboard boxes of tainted perfumes into the trunks of the two squad cars. Oblivious to the steady rain, Lee stands with his arm around Janie Hiller.

"Chief Rowan, Ms. Hiller was unaware of her brother's activities. She thought he was putting pheromones in the perfumes," he says.

"That may be, Mr. Thistleseed, but I still have to arrest her. She did steal all these animals," Chief Rowan says.

"Then may I speak on her behalf?"

"I can give you that, Mr. Thistleseed. Talk to my officer over there. He'll take your statement. Ms. Hiller, let's get you in the car."

When the Chief reaches for Janie Hiller, she pulls back out of his grasp and runs into the woods, right towards Shine who is standing by the SUV.

"Stop!" shouts Chief Rowan.

At that moment, a streak of lightning flashes over the road. Thunder rumbles, making the ground shake, and then there is a loud crack. Looking up, Shine sees another limb separate from the tree. It begins to fall. She jumps away, shielding the civet with her body, and ends up in Janie's path. The women collide, and the limb lands with a crash on top of them.

The nearby men rush to pull the limb away. Seeing the commotion, Graham races in. His strength is equal to that of two men, and he succeeds in pushing it over to the side of the road. By this time, Lee has come to his side. With mounting dread, they look at the women.

Janie Hiller lies with her neck at an odd angle, sightless eyes staring up into the rain. The medical examiner checks for a pulse and pronounces her dead. Moving to Shine, he finds a weak pulse. Her right wrist is broken, and her head is bleeding, but she is alive.

"She likely has a concussion and some broken bones. I—I don't carry medical supplies for living people," the examiner stammers.

"Kenny!" says Graham. He snatches open the car door and finds Shine's medical kit. Sure enough, Kenny has it packed with exactly the right supplies they need to splint Shine's arm and bandage her head. While the M.E. tends to her wounds, Graham begins to sing a blessing way—a Navajo healing song. His voice is strong and plaintive as he rocks back and forth over the woman he loves. He holds his face and hands up to the sky, letting the rain soak his hair and splatter on his glasses.

The sight of the brawny Indian is a wonder to behold. All around, the other men stop and silently watch and listen. He sings until he hears her voice.

"That's pretty, Gray. I love it when you sing," Shine moans.

Graham bends over the woman and tenderly kisses her lips. "And I love it when you speak." Gathering his resolve, he stands up and faces Lee solemnly. "Liahona Thistleseed. I'd like to ask you for the hand of your daughter, Shinehah."

Lee is pleased, but surprised. "This seems rather sudden, Graham. Are you sure?"

"Our existence in this world is fleeting. I don't wish to waste another day without the one I love," Graham whispers, close to tears.

Touched by the suddenness and the formality of his request, Lee simply nods his consent and shakes the man's large hand. Graham kneels beside Shine and takes her unbroken left hand.

"Shinehah Thistleseed. Will you please consent to be my wife?" he asks.

"Yes," she says. "I will gladly be your wife."

Graham lets out an uncharacteristic whoop, and the bystanders cheer. Leaning down again, he reaches under the car and pulls out a tiny bundle.

"I don't have a ring, Shine, but I do have an engagement present." Graham winks and gently places the shivering wet bundle in the crook of her arm. "This little 'kitty' is for you."

CHAPTER FIFTEEN
<u>OLD FRIENDS, NEW FAMILY</u>

AFTER SPENDING THE NIGHT IN TAMPA—part of which was at the hospital, so Shine could be examined and released—Lee, Graham, and Shine are glad to be on the road for home. This being Sunday, they know that Wren will have a huge brunch waiting. The rain has let up, and Graham makes good time on the trip. From their calculations, they should arrive just when everyone else is beginning to sit down. But, of course, they planned it this way.

Shine sleeps much of the way, cradling the rescued civet cub on her lap. "Lovie," as she calls it, is happy to be petted, but it neither purrs nor makes sounds of contentment as other cats do.

"She doesn't purr," Shine says.

"She's not a cat, sweetie. She's a civet—a wild animal," Graham says.

"O.K. I don't have any vet training for a civet. I'll

have to do some research when we get home," she says.

"And until you do that, your little 'Lovie' stays in your cottage. If you let her out, I am afraid she may follow her natural instincts and become wild," Lee says.

"I want to show her to the other kids first," Shine says.

"Not until we find out more about her. She must be inoculated. I do not want any of the children bitten," Lee says.

"Yeah, that's a good idea. She's tame with you, but when she gets a look at that mob of a family, she may get vicious," Graham says.

"Mob of a family?" Lee says. "I can withhold my blessing at any time, you know."

Graham grimaces. "Yes, sir. Point taken. Here we are. Home sweet home."

Graham passes the carport and drives directly to Shine's cottage in the back yard—a barn-style shed with a loft that has been converted into a small house. He reaches into the back seat and takes Lovie from Shine's arms, and then he places the civet on the couch in the little house. After filling a dish with water, he securely closes the door and returns to the car.

"She's all settled until we finish lunch," he says, to which he receives grateful smile from his new fiancé. "She laughed at me, though."

"What?" Shine asks.

"She laughed. Really, she did. You know, like 'ha-ha-ha' laughing."

"Sure, she did. I'm the one with the concussion, and you hear a cat laugh."

"And I'm the clairaudient. Never mind. You'll see when she laughs at you."

"All the more reason for the civet to stay in your house, Shinehah. Your mother can only take so much laughter," Lee says, pulling his mouth into a smirk.

As Graham parks in the carport, he makes a casual observation. "Looks like the Lightfoot crew is here. Hope they leave enough for the rest of us."

When they enter the house, there is an air of excitement. Oddly, the tables are set, but nobody is eating yet. Everyone seems to be crowded into the family room. Lee notices that all the furniture has been pushed back against the walls, and the two-family groups are sitting all around the room, anxiously watching the trio in the doorway.

Police Chief Jack Abernathy stands in front of the fireplace and motions for Lee to join him. As Lee approaches his friend, Kenny passes by him and goes to Shine, gently touching the cast on her hand.

"Did I pack the right stuff?" he asks.

"You did exactly right," Shine says, giving him a hug. "What's going on here?"

Before he can answer, Wren comes over and puts one arm around her daughter's waist and the other around

Graham. "Congratulations," she whispers.

Graham and Shine look at Kenny, who shrugs and grins.

"Will you all please stand," Jack says to the guests assembled in the room.

From the foyer comes the familiar sound of Bill playing the piano. Because the formal living room was converted to Selah's bedroom, the piano had to be moved next to the stairway. The placement in the high-ceilinged room gives the instrument a music hall sound as it resonates through the open space and up the stairs. The musicians of the family, twins Bill and Selah often perform together for their family home evenings, usually with Bill playing and Selah singing or playing the cello.

Adjacent to the family room, the door to Lee and Wren's bedroom opens, and out stroll Dane and Noah. Dane is dressed in traditional Seminole clothing, with the long, colorful patchwork shirt over his slacks. He wears a cloth turban on his head. Noah is dressed, ironically, in his Chief Osceola clothing—minus the war paint. They stop and stand in front of the French doors to the right of the fireplace.

Shine's mouth drops open. "Oh! It's a wedding!" she squeals.

The door between the family room and the foyer opens, and Shelly Thistleseed walks out, wearing her blue and white Sunday dress and carefully holding a smoldering stick of sage. She walks down the center of the room, places the sage in a shell bowl on the fireplace, and goes to stand with her mother.

Behind her walks Fawn Lighfoot, also dressed in traditional Seminole clothing of long patchwork skirt, short sheer shawl, and sporting her famous hair hat. She carries a bowl of something liquid, which she also places on the fireplace. She moves over and stands in front of the French doors to the left of the fireplace.

The music changes, and everyone knows who the next to enter will be. Raven Looking Bird walks into the room, and there is an audible intake of breath as they behold her. She is dressed in the outfit that Fawn made for her. The long patchwork skirt swirls around her yucca fiber moccasins, and the sheer shawl floats near her waist as she moves slowly forward.

She wears a matching set of elegant seed bead earrings, bracelet, and necklaces which catch the sunlight shining through the dormer window high above her in the foyer. The effect is like a fairy tale. All the elements of the universe seem to have come together to make this day special.

Dane's eyes mist as he looks at his bride. The word beautiful cannot even come close. She carries no flowers, but instead holds a fan of grey and white goose feathers, again courtesy of Fawn's pet, Emma. As she comes to the front of the room, she hands her "bouquet" to Fawn.

Dane takes her hand, and they face Jack Abernathy

and Lee Thistleseed. Jack begins the traditional wedding vows. "Dearly Beloved, we are gathered here in the sight of God to unite this man and this woman in holy matrimony..."

At the conclusion of his part, Raven and Dane turn to one another and recite their vows, ending with an exchange of rings.

"What God has brought together, let no man put asunder," Lee says.

The next part of the ceremony consists of the bride and groom each taking a drink of the liquid in the bowl—an herbal potion prepared and blessed by Fawn, Cedar Woman. Then, she takes the feathered fan and the sage and stands before the couple. She uses the fan to direct the smoke over their heads and their bodies, all the way down to their feet. After that, Fawn takes a finger woven sash and wraps the right hands of the bride and groom together.

During these proceedings, Bill plays the music for *"The Lord's Prayer,"* and Selah sings.

"Our Father, who art in Heaven,
hallowed be thy name."

The second phrase is sung by Bill.

"Thy kingdom come,
Thy will be done on earth as it is in Heaven."

The third phrase is sung by a different girl.

"Give us this day our daily bread,
and forgive us our debts as we forgive our debtors."

Noah's head pops up, and he jerks it around to see

into the foyer. He knows this voice well, and he knows the girl to which it belongs—Maria Ramirez. He looks back at Lee but sees only amusement in his face. His heart pounds. *Maria is here!* Maria, with whom he fell in love just weeks ago, and whom he thought he may never see again. Maria, whom he will never let out of his life again, is here, and Noah intends to make her his own.

Selah, Bill, and Maria finish the song together.

"And lead us not into temptation,
but deliver us from evil.
For Thine is the kingdom, and the power,
and the glory, Forever. Amen."

At the song's end, Dane takes Raven in his arms and kisses her for a very long time.

Lee clears his throat. "Family and friends, I give you Dane and Raven Lightfoot."

The room erupts with cheering. Family and friends rush forward to congratulate the bride and groom, as well as Graham and Shine, thanks to Kenny's announcement of their engagement last night. But not Noah. Noah rushes to the foyer to see Maria. He finds her there with Bill and Selah. When he walks up, Bill pulls Maria forward.

"Maria Ramirez. I want you to meet my friend, Noah Lightfoot. He's Chief Osceola at F.S.U. and kinda like my cousin, too," Bill says.

Noah takes her hand and smiles into her eyes, looking for recognition. She gives him a direct stare, turning her head to the side slightly. "Hi there," she says. "Do I know you?"

"Um, maybe. Yeah, well, I don't know," Noah stammers.

"Maria's father is Florida's Governor Robert Ramirez," Selah says. "She sings with us at the junior college sometimes, but she's just transferred to Florida State this semester."

"Maybe we'll see each other around campus," Maria says.

"I'm sure we will. I mean, I hope so," Noah says.

"I'm a music major. I sing and I'm playing the flute in the 'Marching Chiefs' so maybe we can hang out during the games."

"Oh, well, yeah. I'm on the horse, you know. Renegade's the horse, but I don't have to stay on him the whole time. I mean, I can get off the horse and walk around when I'm not actually riding the horse, you know, like during a touchdown or…"

"My gosh, Noah. I think she gets the picture," Bill says rolling his eyes.

"Right, right. Um, Maria, let's get you something to drink, and you can sit by me at the dinner table, if that's alright with you," Noah says, taking her hand and walking her toward the dining room.

Selah and Bill watch Noah awkwardly romancing their friend and laugh. They turn to each other and slap their hands in a "high five" gesture, and then begin singing a tune from *"Fiddler on the Roof."*

"Matchmaker, matchmaker, la da da da;
Dum di dum dum; da di da da..."

* * *

Early the next morning, the newly wed Dane and Raven Lightfoot check out of their hotel honeymoon suite and point their car west. Their decision to visit Raven's mother in Prescott, Arizona comes out of the suddenness of their wedding. Having no time to fly her mother in for the event, they call her and agree to stay for a couple of weeks as her guests. Raven has carefully packed her Seminole outfit and Dane's, as well, so they can give her mother a reenactment of the ceremony.

Knowing the early winter weather in the mountains can become snowy at any time, she also has the foresight to pack them an assortment of socks, gloves, thermal underwear, hats, and coats. Except for his escapade in New York, Dane has spent his entire life in Florida, never having experienced extreme cold; therefore, Raven takes anything she thinks her new husband might need. *I hope it snows,* she thinks. *Won't it be fun to see a Seminole playing in the snow?*

For Dane, the anticipation of two weeks in the mountains is exhilarating. *Imagine, two whole weeks of fresh, clean air. That'll really get my nose back into shape.*

Raven turns in her seat and opens the small cooler on the floorboard. Dane hears the familiar pop and fizz.

"Diet Coke already? It's barely past daylight," he laughs, shaking his head.

"Queasy," she replies, bringing the soda can to her lips.

Dane glances at her. "What are you drinking?"

"Ginger Ale," Raven says. "Your mom weaned me off Diet Coke while she was taking care of me. Said a ginger soda without caffeine was better for a girl in my condition."

"Did you tell her about it?"

"Dane, she's your mother—the Cedar Woman. Nobody has to tell her; she just knows."

"You're right about that, thankfully." He leans over and rubs his hand against her cheek, then rests it on the slight protrusion of her belly.

Raven sighs happily, and then she reaches into her moccasin and pulls out the gold filigreed perfume canister that Dane gave her for their engagement. She presses the top and a fine mist of droplets fans out and onto her neck. Instantly, the scent of vanilla fills the car.

Dane jerks the car to the side of the road and slams it into park, facing her.

"What are you doing?" he cries. "That's poison, Babe!"

Raven pats his hand and laughs. "Relax, Bucko. Your mother threw out the bad stuff, remember? This is one of her special herbal blends. It's a mix of lemon, rose, jasmine, patchouli, iris, and vanilla, of course, in extra-virgin olive oil. Fawn is a master of scent combinations. Probably where you got some of your gift, huh." She caps the bottle and replaces it in her moccasin.

He blows out his breath in relief, and then pulls back onto the highway. "Babe, you're gonna kill me yet!"

"Nah. But thanks for caring." Searching beneath her seat, she takes out her sketch pad and the box of colored pencils he bought her in Tampa. Turning to a blank page, she starts to draw, humming tunelessly as she outlines and shades her picture. When she finishes, she admires her work.

It is a Hopi Kachina—the Sun god. It is circular, like a target, with an outer rim of thirty-two black scallops. They encircle a ring of white, also divided into thirty-two sections, each with a vertical black line running up and down the centers. These are meant to represent the feathers on the actual Sun god mask.

The central circle is divided into an upper and lower hemisphere with a white dashed line. The upper hemisphere is halved by a white dashed line. To the left of the line the area is colored red with a yellow interior; to the right, it is yellow with a red interior. The lower hemisphere is colored blue. Within it, black lines give the indication of two straight-line eyes and a triangular shaped mouth, also colored black.

Dane glances over at the drawing she holds up for his inspection as she describes it.

"These are feathers, and this is the face. These lines are eyes, and here is the mouth," she says. "The Hopi and some Yavapai Indians believe that the Sun god controls the seasons."

"He looks a little sad, don't you think? He's frowning. Why is that?" Dane says.

Raven looks at her picture, and then compares it to the one in the book her mother gave her. Indeed, the mouth of her Sun god image is inverted, giving it the appearance of unhappiness. "I don't know, honey. That's just how he wanted to be drawn," she says.

"Well, if the Sun god's unhappy, then we may be in for some wicked weather," he says.

A chill runs down Raven's back, and she crosses her arms over her stomach protectively.

EPILOGUE

THE KEEPER

BY THE TIME I FINISH collecting the story of Dane—the Bloodhound, the sun is high overhead. It warms my face, and instinctively I close my eyes to keep them from getting damaged. But Mother has already covered my forehead with a cloth. My flute is still clenched between my fingers, and they ache.

Luna," Mother says. "*Que Pasa?* How are you? *Enkv?* OK?"

I am used to the odd mixture of Spanish, English, and Muskogee in her conversation.

"What do you keep?" Mother asks.

"My brother. And now a new sister," I say with a smile.

She cocks her head at me, and I can hear her hair brushing against her cotton blouse. "Noah again?"

"Not this time. It was Dane—the one who was

brought back from beyond the veil of death when Liahona Thistleseed backtracked."

"And Raven?" Her voice is curious. I can tell she is smiling.

"She has become my sister."

"*Mvdo.* It is good. *Andale.* Let's go" she says. She takes my arm and walks me toward our village. I am weak, as always, and exhausted from such a long journey.

"How long, this time?" I ask.

"Three days, daughter. I fed you while you flew," Mother says. We walk a little more, and then she asks, "How many days did you travel?"

I think about it a minute before I answer her. "Three weeks. I traveled three weeks."

"Hmmph. The last time was only a day. You are gone one day for each week. I am afraid for such long journeys." She pulls me closer.

"Mother," I say as I step lightly beside her, "I spoke to a boy in my journey."

"Did he hear you?"

"Yes. And I heard him. I saw him, but he did not see me."

We walk silently for a while. "Mother, I am afraid for my other family," I admit.

"Did you see something else?"

"No. But I know danger is coming. I feel it, and it is so cold."

Mother drapes a shawl around my shoulders. She continues walking again, slowly. After a few steps she stops and embraces me. She kisses the top of my head, and I feel her smile.

"Do not worry, Luna. You are a *hecetv*—a seer. When it happens, you will see it. And whatever it is, your brothers will overcome it."

"It is not my brothers I am worried about. It is my sister, Raven, and her children."

APPENDIX

LANGUAGE TRANSLATIONS

Muskogee Creek Language

The Muskogee Creek language is spoken extensively on the reservations in Oklahoma; however, in the Southeast, there are relatively few native speakers. In the tri-state region of Florida, Georgia, and Alabama, language classes are held in an effort to keep the language from becoming extinct.

The vowels are pronounced as follows:

A=w_A_tch	E=_I_tch	E=s_EE_
I=s_AY_	O=m_OA_n	U=b_OO_k
V=_U_nder	EU=_U_se	UE=b_OY_
VO=n_OW_	Note: vowels are voiced with partially closed, tight mouth.	

Consonants are sounded as follows:

C=ri_CH_	C=ca_TS_	C=_J_am
F=_F_air	H=_H_air	K=bi_K_e
K=_G_o	L=_L_ike	M=_M_an
N=ma_N_	P=_P_ie	P=_B_uy
R=_TLH_ or _HL_ (There is no English equivalent. The sound is much like an attempt to bring forth phlegm)		
S=_S_ee	S=_Z_oo	SK=wi_SH_
SS=wi_SH_	T=_T_ea	T=_D_ie
W=_W_et	Y=_Y_et	

> Note: Consonants are voiced with tight mouths, far back in the throat. The sounds are almost "swallowed."

Muskogee Words, Phrases, and their Meanings

(in order of appearance)

Tuskie Mahaya Haco – Brave Teacher Warrior (proper name)

Hvresse torwv – moon eyes

Heles Pocase – medicine man

Chickee – house (an open structure with a thatched roof)

Coo-Taun Cho-Bee – where the big water meets the land (orig. Hitchiti language)

Pvsktv – fasting celebration

Hal Pa Te – alligator

Sofkee – a corn drink

Hesaketvmese – The One Above (proper name for God)

Taal-holelke – swamp cabbage or sabal palm

Cvke – trickster coyote

Enkv – O.K., alright

Mvdo – It is well; it is good; good; thank you; you're welcome

Hecetv – you see

Spanish Language

Conversational Spanish, in its many forms and dialects, is one of the most widely spoken languages in the world and is prevalent throughout Mexico, Central America, and the United States. Though it varies slightly by regions, it is generally consistent in its pronunciation.

The vowels are pronounced as follows:

A=w_A_tch	E= b_E_d	I =s_EE_
O=m_OA_n	U=b_OO_k	Y =s_EE_
Note: vowels are voiced with open, relaxed mouth.		

Consonants are sounded as follows:

B =_B_ed	C=_C_ow	C=_S_ow
D=_Th_ink	F=_F_un	G=_G_un
H=silent	J=_Ch_ew	K=_K_ick
L=_L_ick	LL=_Y_ard	M=_M_an
N=_N_ow	Ñ=can_Y_on	P=_P_ark
Q/QU=_K_ick	R=ca_RR_y	RR=as _R_, but trilled
T=_T_ake	V=_B_ed	W=_W_ater
X=e_X_cuse	Y=_Y_es	Z=pin_TS_
Note: consonants are voiced with open, relaxed mouth. Hard consonants are explosively voiced.		

Spanish Words, Phrases, and their Meanings

(in order of appearance)

Ojos del Luna – Eyes of the Moon (proper name)

Que Pasa – what is happening?

Andale – let us go

Fragrances

Many fragrances are given French names that correspond to aspects of their formula, such as flowers, spices, base notes, or fixatives. Other names may be colors, gemstones, or a desirable quality. The names in this book are fictional.

Fragrance Names and their Meanings
(in order of appearance)

Lavande - Lavender

DeVanille - Of Vanilla

Diamant - Diamond

Épice d'Asie - Spice of Asia

Eau de (something) - Water of (something)

Chatoyant No. 2 - Shimmering Number 2

Homme DeVanille - Man of Vanilla

VinDoux - Sweet Wine

Les Fleurs du Peintre Français - The Flowers of the French Painter

Romarin - Rosemary

Arômes - Aromas

Céleste - Heavenly

Séduisant - Enticing

PREVIEW the NEXT BOOK in Mickey MorningGlory's sequence of paranormal suspense adventures!

KACHINA

The Snapshot's Story

Book 3 of

The TRACKERS SERIES

* * *

PROLOGUE
PROVO, UTAH~1992

I stink, he thought. And he did. Sweat circled under his arms and around his collar. The pungent odor of fear emanated from his body. No, not fear. Panic. His lips stuck together, chapped from constant licking, and dried snot whitened the outer edges of his nostrils. Flicking his eyes rapidly left and right, he detected no motion; he heard no sounds. Nonetheless, he was not comforted. He shivered, despite the heat in the building. Taking a step closer to the glass display case, he held his breath and fitted the shiny new key into the lock. The nearly imperceptible clicking sound did give him some measure of comfort, and he let his breath out raggedly. He carefully slid the panes apart and took in the contents of the case. Lifting his chin, he acknowledged the spirit captives, and as he gently grasped each carved wooden figurine, he looked it in the eyes and reverently spoke its name.

"*Angwuskatsina,* Crow. *Angwusnusomtaqa,* Crow Mother. *Nata'aska,* Big Mouth Ogre. *So'yokwuuti* , Ogre Woman. *Ewtoto* , Chief. *Ahöla* , Chief's Lieutenant. *Lenangtaqa* , Flute Player. *Poliimana* , Butterfly Maiden. *Kwewu* , Wolf. *Sowi'ingkatsina* , Deer Dancer. *Tsopkatsina* , Antelope. *Sikyaqoqlo* , Artist. *Wupamokatsina* , Guard. *Qaletaqa* , Warrior. *Hee'e'e* , Warrior Maiden. *Koyemsi* , Mudhead Racer. *Tuhavi,* Paralyzed Brother. *Kiisa* , Chicken Hawk Racer. *Kwahu* , Eagle. *Kokopölö*, Humpback. *Pootawikkatsina* , Coiled Plaque Carrier. *Muuyawkatsina,* Moon."

His gloved hand trembled as he reached for the last one. "*Tawa,* Sun," he breathed, adding it to the other spirit beings safely ensconced in protective fabric and bubble wrap. With great care and attention to the photos he had taken of their positions, he filled their places in the display case with expertly crafted duplicates, slid the panels closed, and locked the glass. Then, calm at last, he left the BYU Museum of People and Cultures, cradling in his arms precious cargo belonging to his people.

The Katsinam watched and listened as their mortal

deliverer initiated their escape. They made no noises of disapproval, for they knew they were going home. Only *Tawa* knew what was ahead, and he frowned.

* * *

Across the country in Florida, Raven Looking Bird Lightfoot searched beneath her seat for the sketch pad and the box of colored pencils her new husband, Dane Lightfoot, bought her in Tampa. Drawing would make the trip to Arizona seem shorter. Although Raven was a legitimately gifted artist, her abilities transcended the ordinary and were influenced by her heiroscripting psychic powers, often without her conscious intention.

Turning to a blank page, Raven started to sketch, humming tunelessly as she outlined and shaded her picture. When she finished, she admired her work. It was *Tawa*, the Sun god—a Hopi Kachina, or *Katsina*, as the benevolent spirit being was called in her language. Its face was circular, like a target, with an outer rim of markings meant to represent the feathers on the actual Sun Katsina mask. The central circle was divided into three portions—two upper and one lower. To the left of the center line the upper area was colored red with a yellow interior; to the right, it was yellow with a red interior. The lower hemisphere was colored blue. Within the colored portions of the circle, black lines gave the indication of two straight-line eyes and a triangular shaped mouth, also colored black.

Dane glanced over at the drawing, listening as she

described it.

"These are feathers, and this is the face. These lines are eyes, and here is the mouth," she said. "The Hopi and Yavapai Indians believe that the Sun Katsina controls the seasons."

"He looks a little sad, don't you think? He's frowning. Why is that?" Dane said.

Raven looked at her picture, and then compared it to the one in the book she had received from her mother. The mouth of her Sun god image was inverted, like a scowl.

"I don't know, honey. That's just how he wanted to be drawn," she said.

"Well, if the Sun god's unhappy, then we may be in for some wicked weather," he said

A chill ran down Raven's back, and she crossed her arms over her stomach protectively.

* * *

Hundreds of miles away, my eyes fly open, and I stare at nothing. I know the young newlywed couple. Dane is my brother—one who just returned from beyond the veil of death. Raven is my new sister, and she carries my nephews in her belly.

I am Luna—short for *Ojos del Luna* (as my village family calls me); *Hvresse Torwv* (as my Creek Indian mother calls me). Both names mean the same—Moon Eyes. My eyes are so blue they are almost white, and Mother says that is why I am blind. But when I play my flute, I can see everything in my dream travels. I often travel great distances, and the world is vivid and colorful, with keen sensory perceptions of sound and smell.

I am a "Story Keeper." I remember in great detail what I see on my journeys. The stories I tell are not mine, but I keep them in my memory always, as do I keep all the other stories related to this group of people whose lives intersect mine in a strange and unexplainable way.

This one is hers—the Snapshot's story. It begins the first day of my new sister's married life.

Continue the saga with

KACHINA

The Snapshot's Story

Book 3 of The TRACKERS SERIES

Patent Print Books

ABOUT THE AUTHOR

MICKEY MORNINGGLORY is a former school teacher, storyteller, and performer. Her diverse background includes the *American Federation of Television and Radio Artists (AFTRA), Apalachicola Band of Eastern Creek Indians,* theater, civic light opera, and ethnomusicology. She is a member of *Sisters in Crime (SinC), Society of Children's Book Writers and Illustrators (SCBWI), American Copy Editors Society (ACES),* and *National Association of Independent Writers and Editors (NAIWE).*

Ms. MorningGlory's involvement with indigenous Native tribes has made her *"a friend of many fires."* She crafts The Trackers Series multicultural paranormal mystery books in LIB-B, her "Little Itty-Bitty Barn" writing studio in the Northwest Florida woods. Readers can visit her website at mickeymorningglory-us.com.

Made in the USA
Lexington, KY
13 July 2018